THE GREEN PEARL CAPER

A Damien Dickens Mystery

by

Phyllis Entis

Preface

This is a work of fiction. With the exception of certain historical references, the characters and events described in this novel are products my imagination, or are used fictitiously and are not to be construed as real. While I have taken some liberties with street names and place names, I have tried to be true to the geography and ambiance of the locales that form the backdrop to this story.

I began to write The Green Pearl Caper while participating in Pen to Paper, a drop-in writing workshop hosted by the La Jolla-Riford Branch of the San Diego Public Library and moderated most ably by Diane Malloy. I am indebted to Diane for helping to guide my transition from science writer to novelist. I am grateful for the invaluable aid and support which I received from my husband, Michael Entis, who listened patiently to a read-through of the entire first draft of the manuscript, provided constructive plot suggestions, assisted me in crafting my protagonist's aeronautical adventures, and helped me to comb the manuscript for inconsistencies, errors and copy-edit issues. Thanks also are due to Barbara Bloomfield, Frank Entis, Lorna McKerness, Krystyna Miedzybrodzka, and Elizabeth Porterfield for reading and critiquing my manuscript.

Finally, this book is dedicated to the memory of my parents, Gertrude and Louis Lutsky, from whom I inherited my love for the well turned phrase.

Prologue

I killed Celine. A couple of teenagers found her body last Sunday morning, half-hidden under the Boardwalk, a single bullet hole through her chest. The bullet came from my Smith & Wesson 29, the gun found on the beach not far from where Celine lay.

It wasn't my finger that pulled the trigger. I wasn't there when she died. Even so, I killed her. She came to me for help; I had bailed her out of a tight spot in the past, and she trusted me. But, this time, I let her down. I didn't believe she was really in danger. I screwed up, and Celine paid the price. She was murdered, and it's my fault.

Celine walked into my office on July 16, 1979. Less than one week later, she was dead.

One

I was sitting at my desk late that Monday afternoon, the Sunday edition of The Press, Atlantic City's daily newspaper in front of me. I had the paper open to the Personals section of the classified ads and was staring at a display ad that read, 'Dickens Detective Agency. We find what you're looking for.' The ad was Millie's idea. Her hobby is taking Adult Education classes at the local community college. This semester, the topic was Marketing. "Run it for a week," she had urged me. "It will help to bring in new business. You'll see." I looked at the dateline at the top of the page. Sunday, July 15, 1979. The ad had run for a full week without generating anything more than a few crank calls.

The detective business is an unpredictable racket. Sometimes feast, most times famine. Over the past year, the Dickens Detective Agency had been experiencing a drought. The economy was dicey. With inflation running at more than 13%, consumers weren't buying, and companies were trimming staff, making a severe dent in the demand for employment background checks, a major source of income for us. To make matters worse, a dearth of divorce actions meant that the surveillance business had gone missing, too.

My name is Damien Dickens, and I am a Private Investigator, licensed by the State of New Jersey. I keep an office suite on the second floor of a three-story building on the southwest corner of Atlantic and North Carolina. It's not much of a suite - just an outer office with a filing cabinet and a reception desk for Millie, a small private office for me, and an adjoining washroom. My office overlooks the street; when I open the window, I bask in the aroma of Happy's Bar and Grille, located right below. And there's a parking lot behind the building where I stash my '71 ice-blue Toyota Celica.

Millie Hewitt takes care of the front office. She's about 5'5" tall; her blond hair, china-blue eyes, manicured fingernails, slender build, and fashionable way of dressing scream 'bubble brain' to those who don't know her. But under all the fluff is a spine of steel, a loyal heart and a sharp - if somewhat off-center - intelligence. She walked in one day - I still don't know why - took one look at the stacks of loose papers that tumbled over every horizontal surface, and told me I was hiring her. We didn't discuss her credentials or her salary. She just sat down and went to work. After about an hour of shuffling papers, she came over to my desk, introduced herself, and we shook hands. Millie is more than an employee. She has become a friend, a companion and a confidante. I feel good in her company, even though we must look like Mutt and Jeff together. I'm six inches taller, ten years older, and a few pounds overweight, but she doesn't seem to mind. Nor does it appear to bother her that my sport jacket is always rumpled, my shoes scuffed, and my necktie usually askew. I used to ask Millie from time to time what she saw in me. She would give me a Mona Lisa smile in response and say, "Just because the cover isn't pretty, doesn't mean that the book is not worth reading." Lately, I've stopped asking; I don't know what I'd do if Millie decided to exchange me for a book with a prettier cover.

It was a few minutes after five. Millie had already gone for the day - she had a class that evening - leaving the newspaper behind on my desk, with a note that read, 'Please renew the ad. One week is not a good test.' I had already chucked the note into my waste basket and was about to do the same to the paper, when I heard a gentle tap on my open office door followed by a soft, hesitant voice. "Mr. Dickens?" I looked up and caught my breath. She was beautiful. Not just pretty. Any woman can be pretty with the right hairdo, make-up, and clothes. But this woman was beautiful: silky auburn hair tied in a simple ponytail that swayed gently between her shoulder blades with every move of her head, a long, pearl-smooth neck that disappeared into a simple white tee-shirt stuffed into the waistband of faded blue denims, and a pair of penny loafers on her otherwise bare feet. Her hands and arms were empty of jewelry, though each earlobe sported a small green pearl on a platinum stud. Her fingernails were well-shaped but unpolished. She carried a slender calfskin portfolio case under her right arm, and held the Personals section of the Sunday paper in her left hand. I could see the words 'Dickens Detective Agency' peeking out from between her fingers.

"Mr Dickens?" she repeated, a little more insistently. I looked up into a pair of limpid chocolate brown eyes, gently veiled by a generous endowment of auburn eyelashes, and accented by matching eyebrows. The bridge of her once straight nose had a small bump - the result of one of her youthful indiscretions; the slight smile on her full lips did not extend to her eyes. I suddenly realized that I had been staring, and that Celine knew exactly the effect she was having on me. I cleared my throat and found my voice. "Celine?" I managed. "Sorry. You caught me by surprise."

"Mr. Dickens," she began.

"Damien," I interrupted, "or Dick, if you prefer."

"Damien," she nodded in acknowledgment. "You saved my life when you dragged me out of that Ensenada dive eight years ago. I was furious with my father for sending you after me, and I hated you for bringing me home, even though I knew all along that I needed help." She stopped, took a deep breath and carried on. "Mr. Dickens - Damien - I need your help again." She looked straight at me, her poise contrasting sharply with the urgency in her voice and the anxious, almost hunted, look in her eyes.

I did my best to appear detached and business-like. "Go on," I nodded.

She opened her mouth, then hesitated; her eyes filled with tears, and her entire body shook with enormous sobs. I stood as if on cue, walked around my desk, and touched her on the shoulder. And, before I knew it, she was in my arms, her tears soaking through my shirt. I held Celine until I felt the sobs subside, then guided her back into her seat, handed her a box of tissues, and took my place across the desk from her. I waited while she struggled to regain her composure. When I thought she was ready, I leaned forward. "What's wrong, Celine? How can I help you?"

She thought for a moment, then began with a question. "How much do you know about what happened after you delivered me back to my father?" she asked.

"I know that your father paid me generously for finding and bringing you home," I shrugged. "I don't usually stay in touch with my clients after my job is done."

"Well," she said, "My escapades scared Daddy badly. Badly enough to change his will before he died." She paused to daub her eyes with a tissue, then went on. "Daddy always meant for Sylvia, Susan and me to each inherit equal shares of his business as soon as we turned twenty-one. My sister Sylvia, the oldest, already was managing Sutherland Smokes, although Daddy still remained Chairman of the Board and kept an eye on things. He expected Susan and me to join the company, too, once we finished school. But after my adventure out west, he wanted to make sure of us."

"So, what did he do?"

"Daddy had his attorney, Arnold Barnstable, add a codicil to his will. Until Susan and I turned twenty-five and either earned a graduate degree or joined Sutherland Smokes full time, our shares in the company were to be held in trust by Sylvia, with Barney - Arnold Barnstable - as co-trustee. Susan and I were to receive generous allowances, paid out of our share of the profits, with the balance held in a trust account under Barney's control.

6

Sylvia and Barney retained voting control of our shares until Susan and I fulfilled the conditions of Daddy's will."

"Does anyone else hold any shares in the company?"

"Yes, and that's what brought me here," she nodded. "Daddy put 10% of the shares into a pension fund for the employees. So, in fact, Sylvia, Susan and I each inherited 30% of the company."

"And this pension fund is managed by…"

"Barney. He's also Corporate Counsel and Board Secretary."

Celine paused, and I waited in silence for her to continue. "When I graduated from Harvard with my MBA," she went on, "I gained full voting control of my shares. I chose to work for a consulting firm for a few years to gain some outside experience. When I eventually joined Sutherland Smokes, I decided to understudy Sylvia's husband, Gordon Sethwick - he's CFO. They both claimed to be pleased with my choice, although they tried to discourage me from getting directly involved in the day-to-day accounting. 'Too technical for someone who isn't a CPA,' Gordon would say. I needed to 'dip my toes gently, not dive right in.' I could understand that he might view me as a threat to his position, so I didn't push. I figured time would take care of his objections. Then, a couple of months ago, a delegation of employees came to see me. They suspected that someone was fiddling the books. Business is booming, but the pension fund has been shrinking. They thought I should know."

"Why didn't they speak to Sylvia, or to Arnold Barnstable? Didn't you say that he manages the pension fund?"

"They tried to, but Sylvia and Gordon had gone out of town. And they couldn't get an appointment with Barney."

"So, what did you do?"

"I looked at the books myself. Our sales are at a record high. But our expenses - admin, R&D, marketing - have grown three times as fast. Enough to swallow up all of the profits, and more."

I must have looked confused. High finance was never my strong suit. I left all the arithmetic to Millie. Come to think of it, maybe her math skills weren't so great, either. After all, there was a foot-tall stack of overdue bills sitting on the corner of my desk.

"There was no way that the expenses should have been that high," Celine explained, in response to the look of puzzlement on my face. "We hadn't taken on any new employees, our R&D department was half the size that it had been when Daddy ran the company, and we had cut back on our advertising program."

"So the employees were right?"

"The only possible explanations were either gross incompetence or massive fraud - embezzlement," she said.

"What did you do next?"

"Well, Sylvia and Gordon weren't due back for a couple more weeks, so I went to see Barney. He listened to my story, patted me on the shoulder, and said he'd take care of everything. He suggested that I might have misread the financials - I was still learning the business, he reminded me - and he asked me not to do or say anything further until he had a chance to investigate for himself."

"And did he? Investigate, I mean?"

"He called Sylvia. She flew home the next day and confronted me. She was furious. How dare I go behind her back, she asked. How dare I take the side of a few disgruntled employees? Did I want out? She'd be happy to oblige. 'Name your price,' she told me."

Two

"I don't remember exactly what I said to Sylvia," Celine continued, "but I managed to calm her down. I never really wanted to work at Sutherland's to begin with; I only joined the company to honor Daddy's wishes. But I won't be forced out. And I won't see the company destroyed. I have my son's inheritance to protect."

"Your son?" I asked. "But, I thought..." My words trailed off as she held my gaze, her eyes glittering in their determination - the look of a lioness protecting her cub.

"Just because I left my son, don't think for one minute that I abandoned him, Damien." Her voice trembled with suppressed emotion. "I entrusted him to my old nanny and her husband, and I've stayed in contact with them. With him." She held up a hand to forestall my next question. "He doesn't know that I'm his mother," she explained. "He calls me Aunt Celine. The only people who know the truth are his foster parents. I haven't even told Susan."

"What about the boy's father?"

"I never told him. I thought that I might, someday, but ..." She paused, gesturing vaguely with her right hand, then picked up the thread of her narrative.

"Anyway, things seemed to settle down after that. Sylvia went out of her way to make up for her outburst. She had Gordon sit down with me to 'explain' the books. And they invited me to their place for dinner whenever Susan was in town - she's going to college in Vermont. But I always had the feeling that I was being watched; I never got to speak to Barney again. He's always tied up when I call, or on his way to a meeting when I simply drop in on him. And I've never had more than a moment alone with Susan. Either Sylvia or Gordon is always with us."

"Just one happy family?" I ventured. Celine didn't take any notice. She was completely caught up in her story now.

"Last week," she went on, "Gordon laid off all of the members of the employee delegation that had approached me about the financial discrepancies. Some of them had been with the company for more than twenty years. He tried to pass off the firings as a reorganization - a cost-cutting measure. But I knew better. I confronted him; he told me to mind my own business if I knew what was good for me. Since then, I've had a couple of strange phone calls at home, even though my number is unlisted - dead air when I first pick up, followed by heavy breathing." Celine looked straight at me. "Damien," she said, her voice almost a whisper, "I think that he's the one behind all of this. I think he has Sylvia fooled. I believe that Gordon Sethwick is bleeding the company dry."

Celine sat up straighter, determination radiating from her eyes, mouth and spine. "I'm not going to stand aside while my father's most loyal employees get shafted," she declared. "And I'm not going to allow Gordon Sethwick to steal my son's future." She paused to remove a large brown envelope from her leather portfolio, turning it over and over in her hands as she continued. "I need your help, Damien. I need to get to the bottom of this."

"What can I do that you can't?" I wondered. "You have access to all the records, don't you?"

"You can get in to see Arnold Barnstable, for one thing," she said. "He seems to be avoiding me. He and Sylvia are pretty tight - much closer than she and I are. If Gordon is behind this, Barney will want to protect Sylvia's interests. Tell him what's going on. Ask him, on my behalf, to arrange an outside audit of the company's books. He's still trustee for Susan's share and for the pension fund. If he and I both insist, then Gordon will have to comply."

"OK," I nodded. "What else?"

10

She shook her head and smiled slightly. "You're the detective, Damien. You figure it out."

"Where can I reach you?"

She took out a business card, turned it over and wrote a couple of numbers on the back before handing it to me. "I'm driving up to Burlington tonight to see Susan and tell her everything. I want her to meet Arthur and his foster parents. Just in case something happens to me. The first phone number is my apartment here in town. I'll be back in a day or two. If you need to reach me before then, the number with the 802 area code is Susan's. You can call me there."

I stood as I took the card from her hand. "I'll do the best I can for you, Celine. You can count on that."

"I know," she said, then handed the envelope to me. "This contains a detailed report of everything I've been able to find out. It includes a list of all the fired employees, with their addresses and phone numbers. And there's one more thing."

I raised my right eyebrow in query - a little trick that took me years to perfect.

"You'll find a sealed envelope in there. Please don't open it." She paused and drew a sharp breath before continuing. "Unless I'm dead. It contains a talisman that will introduce you to Arthur's foster parents, their address, and a sealed letter addressed to my son's father. I'll leave it to you to judge whether or not he deserves to know that he has a son."

It all sounded melodramatic - like something you'd read in a detective story. I wondered briefly whether I was being had. But she seemed sincere as hell, so I agreed. I'd see Barnstable. Celine would get her audit, and I'd get my fee. And the phone company would get paid. Celine's eyes brightened with grateful tears when I accepted the envelope from her. She kissed me on the cheek as she took

11

her leave, a faint hint of perfume trailing in her wake, and her ponytail swaying jauntily between her shoulder blades as she made a right turn out of my office to head down the hall to the elevator.

I made a photocopy of the information Celine left with me before sealing the entire package of originals into a clean envelope. I spent the rest of the afternoon reading through her report and contacting some of the people on the list of fired employees. Before leaving the office, I locked my copy of the information, including my own notes, in my desk drawer. On my way home, I stopped by the main post office and sent off the originals by registered mail. I wanted them in a safe place. If Celine was correct, I especially wanted to ensure that the mysterious sealed envelope would be safe and secure.

The next morning, I called Barnstable's office and set up an appointment for Wednesday, July 18th. I wanted to give Celine a chance to get up to Burlington and speak to Susan. Or to change her mind - I'm not sure which. Also, I needed to refresh my memory on the history and habits of the Sutherland family. Fortunately, the local library had a complete microfilmed archive of The Press. I searched back through the archives to the first mention of Arthur Sutherland - his 1939 marriage to Lois, his simultaneous adoption of Lois's five-year old daughter, Sylvia, and a vague reference to an older child who was 'away at school' and unable to attend the wedding ceremony. This announcement was followed, over time, by brief mentions of Lois's death in 1944, Arthur's marriage to Julia Chesterton in 1946, the births of Celine in 1949 and Susan in 1953, and Julia's death from influenza later that same year. Sylvia's marriage to Gordon Sethwick on December 26, 1969 was covered in great detail in the society column, under the headline, "Tobacco Heiress Weds." I made note of the relevant dates, then drove out to May's Landing, the county seat, and obtained copies of the birth, marriage, adoption and death records for all the various members of the Sutherland family.

On Wednesday morning, I presented myself to Barnstable's secretary promptly at nine o'clock. After the usual pleasantries, exchanged over the richest cup of coffee I had ever sipped, Barnstable and I got down to business. I told him about my visit from Celine, and presented him with a letter of introduction that she had given me, naming me as her agent. I emphasized her concern that someone - I avoided mentioning names - might be embezzling money from the family business. And I asked him, in her name, to request an independent audit. Although Barnstable appeared taken aback, his reply was as smooth as the cream in my coffee. "I find it very hard to believe," he pronounced, "that either Sylvia or her husband would steal from the company. I'm nonplussed that Celine would ever harbor such suspicions. However, I shall certainly present Celine's request at the next meeting of the company's Board of Directors."

"And when do you expect that to take place?" I asked.

He checked his calendar. "The next meeting is scheduled for July 23rd, the Monday after the 'Christmas in July' charity ball."

I thanked him, drained my coffee cup - I wasn't going to waste a single drop of that elixir - and left his office. As I walked back to my car, two questions kept buzzing in my brain. Why did Barnstable choose to pretend that he was unaware of Celine's suspicions? And why did he assume that she suspected her sister and brother-in-law?

Three

It was late Saturday afternoon on July 21st. Celine had returned from Vermont the night before, and we had agreed to meet Sunday morning to go over my progress. Only, I didn't have much to report. Following my meeting with Barnstable, I'd spent the last couple of days interviewing several former Sutherland employees. Not a single person on Celine's list was willing to corroborate her story, although one old-timer alluded to some concern about his early retirement package being withdrawn if he revealed company information. I was feeling hot and frustrated. The radio - tuned to WMID - reported the temperature at 81°, but there was no breeze, and I could feel the sweat tracing a channel from my armpits down to my belt. I walked over to the washroom sink and splashed cold water on my face.

When I returned to my desk, I could hear the sound of high-heeled shoes clicking along the linoleum tile floor of the hallway to the accompaniment of the muted swoosh of a rope of pearls swaying back and forth across an amply endowed chest. The door to my office swung open, and there stood Sylvia Sutherland. THE Sylvia Sutherland. The CEO of Sutherland Smokes. And let me tell you - Sylvia Sutherland smoked. She was dressed for Christmas - on her way to the 'Christmas in July' charity ball, I found out later - and completely decked out in poinsettia red, except for her emerald green four-inch heels, her emerald-studded evening bag, and the longest rope of half-inch diameter emerald-green pearls I had ever seen - a perfect color match for her shoes and bag. Who but Sylvia would think to wear a rope of perfectly matched Tahitian green pearls? Who but Sylvia could afford to?

"Damien Dickens?" Her voice was crisp and clear - all business.

"That's me," I replied.

"You know who I am." A statement, not a question.

"I worked for your father," I reminded her, waving her into a chair. "What can I do for you?"

"We have a problem," she began, leaning forward briefly to pass a folded sheet of paper across my desk for me to read. Then she leaned back in her chair, brushing her shoulder-length honey-blond hair away from her ears to reveal a pair of green pearl earrings set in miniature platinum oyster half-shells.

"We?" I raised my right eyebrow. "What problem do we have?"

"Not what," she replied. "Who. My sister. Celine. Read that and you'll understand."

I unfolded the paper she handed to me and read, 'Steel Pier. Tonight at 11:15. Bring the cash.' I handed the paper back to her. "What's this about?"

"Celine's gone off the rails." Sylvia paused, took a tissue from her evening bag, daubed her eyes, and discarded the tissue in my wastepaper basket before continuing. "She's accused my husband and me of malfeasance - of milking profits from the company. It's total nonsense, of course, but she won't listen to reason. I understand she even hired you to look into the matter on her behalf." She paused to give me an opportunity to corroborate her last statement.

"Go on," I replied, keeping my tone non-committal. This seemed to fluster her briefly, but she rallied.

"Mr. Dickens," she continued, her posture ramrod-straight. "I think Celine is back on drugs. She's been behaving erratically these last few weeks. She turns up at the office late, if she shows her face at all. Her work is error-strewn, and she's claiming that my husband and I are out to get her. She's become defensive to the point of paranoia. And cash has been disappearing from the office safe. A lot of cash."

I still wasn't sure where Sylvia was going with this. "And what do you want from me?"

"I want you to stop encouraging her fantasies. I want you to tell her that there is no basis in fact for her allegations. And I want you to intercept her at the Steel Pier tonight. I think she's meeting with whoever is supplying her. I want it stopped."

"Then why not call the cops?"

"Because I will not have the Sutherland name sullied by scandal. I want this handled quietly. I want you to rescue her from her own recklessness. You did it once before; you can do it again."

"You want a lot," I observed.

"I'm prepared to pay a lot."

"How much?"

"One thousand dollars. In advance. For one night's work." Sylvia unzipped her bag again, this time to extract a check for $1,000 made out to 'Cash,' which she placed on the desk in front of me. "Will you do it?"

My nose was twitching, and the hairs on the back of my neck were standing to attention - always a sign of trouble. Also, I had promised Millie dinner at Happy's followed by a movie. We were going to take in 'Moonraker,' the latest James Bond film. But this was Celine we were talking about. Regardless of whether or not Sylvia was feeding me bullshit, Celine was in trouble. I had no choice. I picked up the check, folded it carefully in half, and inserted it into my billfold. "Understand me, Sylvia," I said as I stood to usher her out. "I make no promises, except that I'll do my best to intercept her tonight. As for the rest, I'll have to talk to Celine before I decide whether or not to walk away from the job she hired me to do."

I met Millie for dinner as planned, but begged off the movie, explaining that something had come up in the Celine Sutherland case that I needed to look into that night. I dropped Millie off at her apartment, promised to fill her in on Monday morning, then drove to a public parking lot near the Steel Pier. It was just after 10pm, and I spent about a half hour strolling up and down the Boardwalk, searching out a good spot from which to watch for Celine. The crowd was light for a Saturday night, and most of the pedestrians were milling about the entrance to the Resorts Casino Hotel, the Atlantic City Boardwalk's first - and, for the moment, only - casino. The Resorts had opened in May 1978 on the site of the old Haddon Hall Hotel, long a Boardwalk landmark. The casino was a big draw for day-trippers from New York City, who arrived by the busload in mid-morning, complete with coupons for the all-you-can-eat lunch buffet, and departed before dinner time in those same busses, heavier in the belly but much lighter in the wallet.

I found a little alcove between two buildings that furnished me with an unobstructed view of the area around the Steel Pier, and settled in to wait. For what, I wasn't quite sure. The street lamps cast eerie shadows through the fog that was slowly encroaching on the shoreline. I could hear my heart beating above the sound of the incoming tide. In the distance, a clock tower chimed eleven. I peered out from my hiding place and saw two people coming toward me from the direction of the casino. The woman appeared the worse for wear, and was being half-carried by her male companion, her head buried in his shoulder. They disappeared from view before reaching my position - probably heading for the beach in search of some privacy, I figured.

The clock tower chimed again; eleven-fifteen, according to my Casio wristwatch with the little built-in light that drained its battery but allowed me to check the time no matter where I was. As I moved out of the

18

shadows for another look down the Boardwalk, I heard a muffled noise behind me. I turned in time to see a blur out of the corner of my eye. That same instant, I felt a sharp blow on the side of my head, followed by the sensation of the Boardwalk rising to meet my nose, as everything around me went dark.

When I awoke, the sun was slowly breaking through the morning fog, like a flood light on a rheostat that was gradually being cranked up. I could hear a rhythmic tapping sound over the susurrus of the surf. I turned my head, groaning, and was greeted by a highly polished black shoe rhythmically tapping the planks of the Boardwalk about three inches from my face. The shoe belonged to a leg encased in blue, which in turn was attached to a cop - a rookie cop from the look of him, all spiffed and puffed up with importance, his billy club beating against his leg in counterpoint to the tapping of his shoe.

"On a bender, Pop?" the rookie sneered. "This is no place to sleep it off. Stand up and show me some ID."

An unyielding hand that attached itself firmly to my shirt collar dragged me to my feet. I stood, swaying, and dusted myself off. "You've got it all wrong," I told him, fighting the swarm of bees that had taken up residence inside my skull and were trying to get out through my eyes and ears. "I was slugged. I'm a private investigator, and I'm on a case."

"Sure you are," he nodded. "Sure you are. Let's see that ID." I reached for my wallet, where I keep my driver's permit and PI license. But my hip pocket was empty. And I knew by the absence of its weight that my Smith & Wesson 29 was missing from its shoulder holster, too.

"I'm takin' you in to dry out, Pop."

This guy was starting to bug me. "I'm on a case," I protested. "I already told you that. Someone slugged me from behind."

"Sure you are. Sure they did." This rookie had been watching too many old movies - the ones where the cops pretend to believe you in order to lull you into submission. "You can tell your story to the judge in the morning," he added. The rookie took his eyes and his hand off me for a moment in order to reach for the set of handcuffs that was dangling from his leather belt. I saw my chance. I stumbled against him, jostling both the cop and the cuffs to the ground, and sprinted south. I turned off the Boardwalk at North Carolina, and ran half a block before ducking into a narrow alley between two buildings. And hit a wall. Dead end. I could hear the sound of the cop's shoes on the pavement. He would be onto me at any moment. I looked around and spotted a trash dumpster. Any port in a storm, I told myself. I unlatched the security bar that was resting across the lid, scrambled inside, and pulled the top down over me. I waited, holding my breath against the stench of rotting garbage. His footsteps slowed as they approached the alley. Tap. Tap. Tap. He was nearly at the dumpster. I burrowed down into the trash, hoping he wouldn't see me if he looked inside. I heard the creak of a hinge as the lid was lifted, and saw a crack of light, followed by the sound of liquid trickling into the bin. The lid dropped shut, and there was a squeal of protesting metal as the hinged security rod on the outside of the dumpster was rotated back into the latched position. I was trapped. The last thing that I remember before I passed out was the sickly-sweet smell of chloroform that mingled with, then overwhelmed, the stink of the garbage under which I was buried.

Four

I was up to my neck in refuse. I felt the dumpster bin rise, then start to tilt forward in an arc, making mechanical, clanking noises as though it was about to fail. I groped around desperately for a handhold. But before I could find something to grab onto, the bin flipped over completely, and I was flung through the air, buffeted by boxes, bottles and nondescript bundles. I struggled to free myself from the pile of trash in which I had landed, but the garbage behaved like quicksand, and I succeeded only in trapping myself further. There was a loud 'clunk' as the bin returned to its place in the alley; at the same time, a tarp swung into position over my head. Then I heard the grind of shifting gears, and a series of warning beeps as the truck began to back up. I was on my way to the town dump along with the rest of the trash.

The truck turned as it backed out of the alley, paused briefly, then moved forward with a jerk. We traveled about a block, made a right turn, and almost immediately came to a halt - for a traffic light, I figured. After about a minute, we started up again. The truck trundled along, making the occasional left or right turn, which caused the trash to shift under and around me. As I flailed about to free myself, I noticed that there was an unfamiliar lump in my jacket pocket. I pulled out the object and tried to examine it under the feeble shafts of light that were flickering through some gaps in the tarp. It appeared to be an evening bag. I managed to reach into my trouser pocket for my key ring, on which I keep a miniature flashlight. The narrow beam from the penlight reflected and sparkled against the bag's jeweled surface.

I felt the truck stop again, and the compartment in which I was riding began to tilt. I had just enough time to tuck the evening bag back into my jacket pocket for safekeeping before I found myself sliding out of the truck. In barely more than an instant, I was knee deep in a mound of freshly dumped trash at the municipal landfill. I scraped and stumbled my way off the mountain of garbage and back onto *terra firma*. Crouching down on my haunches with my back leaning against a convenient chain link fence, I pulled the evening bag out of my jacket, undid its zipper, and looked inside. My head was still swimming from the effects of the chloroform and the dump truck ride, but I could make out the letter 'S' embroidered daintily into the green silk lining with silver colored thread. The bag was empty, except for a single earring - a perfect green pearl nestled on a miniature platinum oyster half-shell. I recognized that earring. It looked just like the ones that Sylvia Sutherland was wearing when she came to my office.

I felt eyes upon me, and looked up to see a couple of deadbeats watching me. "This is our turf," one of them growled, waving his fist in my general direction. "Get outta here!" I needed no further prodding. I stuffed the evening bag back into my pocket and headed for the nearest street corner to get my bearings. I was at the top of Maryland Avenue, within shouting distance of the Atlantic City Marina and about a mile or so from my office. My Casio wristwatch, bless its rugged little heart, informed me that it was 8:33am on Monday, July 23, 1979. I had lost more than twenty-four hours trapped inside that damn dumpster bin. I limped off in the direction of Atlantic and North Carolina, keeping to the back alleys as much as possible. I hoped to make it all the way to my office, where I kept a spare wallet, without being spotted. For once, luck was with me. I went around to the back of the building and took the service staircase to the second floor.

"Dick!" Millie's face registered her shock at my appearance as I stumbled into the outer office. "What happened to you? Where have you been? A Mr. Sethwick has been looking for you; he's in your office now. He didn't believe me when I told him that I didn't know where you were."

"Shit," I muttered, as I spotted a 6'2" male version of Sylvia Sutherland blocking the doorway to my office. He was dressed in a midnight-green three-piece business suit; his French-cuffed shirt was white with green pinstripes, and his necktie was green, with narrow white diagonal stripes. His platinum cufflinks and tie tack each bore a solitary green pearl on an oyster half-shell. "Dickens," he said, his voice and manner abrupt. "Where is she?"

"Where's who?"

"Celine." He glared at me, fists clenched. "Celine Sutherland. My sister-in-law. She's disappeared. Where is she?"

"How the hell should I know?" I flared at him. "I've just spent the last thirty-six hours in a dumpster bin."

That stopped Sethwick in his tracks for a moment. He looked me up and down, an expression of disgust on his face. "Dickens, you stink to high heaven," he proclaimed before continuing to harangue me over Celine's mysterious absence. I spent the next ten minutes trying to convince him that I had no idea where she was, and finally managed to hustle him out of my office. My head was pounding, my clothes would have been rejected by Goodwill, and Gordon Sethwick was right about one thing, anyway. I stank. I also needed to think. It didn't take a Philip Marlowe to figure out that something was wrong with this picture. Someone was playing me for a fool. But who? What was their game? How did the evening bag and earring figure in all this? And why pick on me?

I heard a hissing sound and looked up to see Millie spraying air freshener around her desk. I could take a hint. I headed for the door. "Where are you going, Dick?" Millie asked, her face furrowed with concern.

"Home," I grunted as I closed the door behind me, the hiss from the aerosol can following me into the hallway. I limped back down the stairs and out the rear door of the building, and slunk along back alleys and side streets until

I reached the public parking lot where I had left my Celica on Saturday night. I clambered in, rolled down the windows, and started for home. Maybe a shower, a nap, a change of clothes, and a stiff Scotch would relieve the pounding in my head.

Home is a 600-square foot one-bedroom walk-up on the third floor of the Carver Hill Apartments about ten blocks from the office. By the time I pulled into the parking lot - seven minutes by my Casio - the interior of the Celica reeked as badly as I did. I locked the car out of habit, but left all the windows open in the faint hope that at least some of the stench would dissipate by the time I returned. I figured that the aroma would be enough to deter anyone from trying to steal the car. I entered my apartment building by the back door and trudged up two flights of stairs. One nap and two showers later, I was in my favorite chair, bath towel wrapped around my waist, sipping my second double Scotch, and staring at the evening bag that was perched on the coffee table in front of me. When the doorbell rang, I heaved my reluctant body into a standing position, walked over to the door, and peered through the peephole. The police badge that was brandished in my field of view obstructed the face of its wielder. I strode to the coffee table, grabbed the evening bag, and shoved it under the cushion of my chair. The doorbell rang again. "Open up, Dickens. We know you're in there." I knew that voice; it belonged to Sergeant Conan Sherlock of the Atlantic City Police Department. We had a history, Sherlock and I, and it wasn't a pretty one.

We had both attended Atlantic City Senior High. He was a jock, breezing through high school on the strength of his football prowess; I was a plugger, struggling to achieve and maintain a B-minus average. We graduated the same year. He entered the Police Academy after graduation; I decided to give college a try. Ocean County Community College was cheap and close; I could afford the tuition and live at home. I chose Psych as my major and, when I attended my first lecture in criminal psychology, I realized what I wanted to do with my life. I completed my diploma in record time and applied to the Atlantic City Police Academy. Upon graduation, I was given my first assignment - walking a beat with a veteran of the ACPD. Constable Conan Sherlock.

We patrolled together for a couple of years, until I saw Sherlock rough up a teenage gang member 'to teach him respect for the law' once too often. My conscience kicked in, and I reported him. Sherlock received a promotion; I got a punch in the nose. I stuck with the Department while my broken nose healed, then went to work for Sutherland Smokes as a security guard until I could afford to strike out on my own as a PI. It was more than ten years since I'd left the Department, and there was still bad blood between Sherlock and me - between a lot of the veteran cops and me for that matter - but we cooperated when it was in our mutual interest to do so.

The doorbell rang a third time, followed by the sound of a heavy set of knuckles rapping on the door. "Keep your shirt on," I called out. "I just got out of the shower." I exchanged the towel for a pair of trousers before opening the door, and stood with my hand on the knob as I watched Sherlock lumber into my apartment, followed by Lieutenant Holmes from Homicide. I hadn't seen Sherlock for a few months. He'd put on about ten pounds, and his uniform was struggling to cope with the change. Sherlock was short - about 5'8" from the soles of his scuffed shoes to the top of his officer's cap - and weighed about 190 pounds. His hair had lost the battle with his scalp at least half a decade ago, and he combed a few remaining strands of long hair over the top of his head to camouflage his bald spot. James Holmes was a beanpole by comparison. He was 6'1" and weighed just 170 pounds. His suit hung loosely on his lanky frame, the sleeves of his jacket and legs of his trousers about an inch too short for the current style. His full head of salt-and-pepper hair was shaped in a

25

crew-cut. I hadn't crossed paths with Holmes before - he had been recruited from the NYPD in November 1978 to head up Homicide - but I knew him by reputation as a no-nonsense cop with a strong sense of right and wrong.

I reached out and patted Sherlock's pot belly where it spilled slightly over his gun belt. "Put on a little weight?"

"Put a sock in it, Dickens," Sherlock growled. As usual, the man had no sense of humor. "Where were you Saturday night between ten p.m. and two a.m.?"

"Who wants to know?" I riposted.

"I do," Lt. Holmes interjected with quiet authority. "Where were you?"

"Out on a case, if you must know," I temporized. "Why?"

"We're asking the questions here," Sherlock snapped.

The hair on the back of my neck was prickling again, and my head was starting to pound. I whirled on him. "But I don't have to answer them if I don't want to, Sherlock," I retorted. "So why don't you take your overstuffed uniform and its contents out of my apartment and let me get back to my Scotch."

"Mr. Dickens," Holmes inserted himself between Sherlock and me. "This is a homicide investigation. We've received a tip that you were seen in the vicinity of the murder scene. Please answer the question."

Holmes was trying the 'Good Cop/Bad Cop' routine. He had it down pat, but I wasn't buying. "Look, Lieutenant," I replied. "I told you. I was out on a case. Now, if you'll excuse me, I have things to do." I herded the cops out the door and locked it behind them, just as the phone rang. With a glance of longing at the glass of Scotch that was still sitting beside my easy chair, I answered. It was Millie.

"Dick, two cops are here. They want to search the place. I told them they couldn't without a warrant, but they're sticking around. They refuse to leave."

"Did they say what they're looking for?"

"No, not a word. They just came in, flashed their badges in my face, and said they wanted to search. When I told them they couldn't, they made growling noises, pushed past me, and sat themselves down in your office. They refuse to leave." Millie was starting to repeat herself - never a good sign.

"OK," I told her. "Listen. Call Gus." I stopped and thought a moment. "Or better still, tell them to leave immediately, or you'll have our attorney press charges against them for trespassing and illegal search. Then pick up the phone to call Gus. I bet they'll hightail it right out the door before you finish dialing his number."

"And that way, we won't have an attorney's bill to pay, right?" I could hear Millie's nod of understanding.

"Right. Hold the fort, Millie. I'll be there as quick as I can."

I hung up the phone, inhaled the rest of the Scotch, shrugged into a clean shirt, and headed for the door. Stopping abruptly, I strode back to the chair in which I had stashed the evening bag, pulled the bag from under the cushion, stuffed it into my jacket pocket, and left. Millie was expecting me, but there was something I needed to do first.

Five

I galloped down the stairs and out the back door. After threading my way between the parked cars in the lot behind my building, I clambered into my Celica and took off, only to come to a grinding halt at the corner. When the red light finally changed to green, I executed a noisy and highly illegal U-turn, headed down S. Tennessee Ave., and turned right onto Baltic. Three blocks into the seediest part of Atlantic City, I parked the car, walked over to Atlantic Avenue, turned left, and came to a halt on the sidewalk across the street from Benny's pawn shop.

It had been three years since I'd last seen Benny. I had been hired by an insurance company to trace some stolen jewelry; my investigation led me to 1736 Atlantic Avenue, then led Benny to prison for dealing in stolen property. The street hadn't changed much since I was last there. The bar on the corner looked a bit more run down, and the lettuce in the window of the mom-and-pop store next to it was a little more wilted. I crossed Atlantic, stopped in front of Benny's shop next door to the grocery store, and looked up at the sign. It hadn't been done any favors by the wind-driven sand and rain over the years, but I could still make out the time-honored symbol of three balls, and the faded lettering, 'Short term loans. Articles bought and sold. Benedetto Caravaggio, Prop.' The contents of the pawnshop window were as weatherbeaten and nondescript as the sign: faux antiques, wanna-be heirlooms, dusty fiddles, tarnished trombones, tubas and trumpets abandoned to their fate by disillusioned musicians, and one elegant, silver French horn that was perched on a high shelf in a corner of the window, staring disdainfully down at its shabby companions.

I opened the door and walked in. A bell rang faintly in a back room, and Benedetto Caravaggio, Prop. slipped out from behind a curtain. Though Benny and I hadn't seen each other since I had testified at his trial, I knew he

29

recognized me. And I would have known him anywhere. He was as shabby and dusty as the contents of his store - about 5'7" tall, with sparse, dirty gray hair that matched the color of his eyes, a two-day growth of dark gray beard that contrasted eerily with his permanent prison pallor, and a gloomy, downcast demeanor.

"Hi, Benny," I greeted him. "When did you get out of the joint?"

"About a year ago, no thanks to you," he replied. "You can't touch me, Dickens," he added defensively. "I'm legit."

"Sure, Benny," I nodded. "And I'm the Pope. But you still have contacts in the club. You know which club I mean, don't you - the fencing club that doesn't use swords?"

"What if I do?" he asked.

I tossed the evening bag on his counter. "I want to know if this is hot. Also, what it's worth," I explained. "There's an earring inside that I'm curious about, too."

"That'll cost you a C-note," he growled.

"OK, payable on receipt of the info."

Benny reached for his jeweler's loupe, screwed it into his left eye socket, and examined the bag. "Is this some kind of joke?" He looked up and glared at me. His erstwhile pasty face sported a bright red spot over each cheekbone. "You owe me a hundred bucks," he said. "This bag is stone cold - not even worth stealing. I can buy it for ten bucks in any novelty store on the Boardwalk."

"And the earring?" I asked.

He unzipped the bag, removed the earring, and peered at it through his loupe. "Fake. Cracker Jack prize."

"You're sure?" I probed. "No chance you could be mistaken?"

"Not a chance in hell! Now cough up that C-note and get out of my shop."

Sighing, I pulled five twenties out of my wallet and laid them on the counter. None of this was making sense. I could have sworn that the bag and earring were the real McCoy. I didn't know what Benny's game was, but I couldn't risk having the items found on me, in my apartment, or at the office. I decided to appeal to Benny's better instinct - his love of an easy buck."Tell you what, Benny," I said. "There's another fifty in it for you if you'll hold onto this bag and keep your mouth shut about it. I'll either come back for it myself or I'll send Millie Hewitt. But no one else gets it. Understand?"

"On the level?" he asked suspiciously.

"Of course!" I was properly indignant. "I'm always on the level. Didn't you know?"

"When do I get the fifty?"

"When you hand the items back over to Millie or me."

A sly smile played across Benny's face. "How about half in advance?"

"No way," I replied. "You've already got a hundred bucks from me for thirty seconds of work. That's enough of an advance."

"OK, Dickens," he relented. "I'll hold these in my back room. Here's a pawn ticket for Miss Hewitt to use if she comes to pick them up. Just don't forget - you promised me fifty bucks for this."

My head was spinning as I drove away from Benny's. Ten dollar bag? Fake pearl earring? I was sure that the bag and earring were twins to the ones that Sylvia had flaunted in my office. Maybe my brain was still addled from inhaling the heady mixture of chloroform and rotting trash. Millie was expecting me, but she'd have to wait. I needed to figure out what was going on. I drove back to the public lot near the Steel Pier, left the car there, and crossed onto the Boardwalk. As I turned south toward the location where I had been slugged on Saturday night, I spotted a souvenir shop and dropped in. Piled helter-skelter in a bin under a sign that read '$10. All Sales Final' I found a heap of evening bags decorated with green plastic sequins. They looked nothing like the bag that I had just left with Benny. I picked one up and tried to undo the zipper, which caught twice on loose threads. When I finally managed to open the bag, the unlined interior bore signs of having been assembled by an amateur. A ragged paper tag sewn into one of the seams read "Made in China."

"Hey, Bud," a raspy voice called out. "You open it, you own it. That'll be ten bucks."

I fished a ten-dollar bill out of my wallet and placed it on the counter. I thought for a moment, then added a second sawbuck and grabbed a souvenir baseball cap from a rack near the cash register. I put on the hat, pulling the beak low over my eyes, stuck the evening bag in my pocket, and headed for a bench on the Boardwalk across from the Steel Pier. From there, I had a perfect view of the burnt-out ramshackle remains of what was once the jewel in Atlantic City's crown. I marked my progress through youth by the changes from summer to summer in the rides and attractions on the Pier. I still recall the first time I saw the Incredible Diving Horse. I was even in the audience on the day that the horse decided to perform his dive without waiting for the daredevil beauty whose job it was to soar through the air on his back. As a teenager, I squired my dates up and down the Pier's midway, showing off my skill at the shooting galleries and the games of strength. I remember a December day in 1969 when the news of a fire at the Pier spread through town as rapidly as the flames that consumed a portion of the structure. And how could I forget the solemn pronouncements in 1976 of 'the end of an era' when the Steel Pier was closed forever. Today, only seagulls and cops were drawn to this Atlantic City landmark; the gulls were busy picking at the coating of barnacles on the pilings that support what's left of the structure. The cops were picking away at a crime scene.

I sat and watched for about a half hour. I was just about to stand up and walk back to my car when I saw Lt. Holmes arrive, Sherlock following in his wake. The homicide team swarmed to Holmes like iron filings to a magnet. I could see him nodding as, one by one, the officers reported on their findings. He turned and strode in the direction of the Boardwalk, the uniforms trailing behind him. Almost immediately after he disappeared from my view, I heard a shout from near the shoreline, where a couple of crime team members had been rooting around with metal detectors and sand rakes. One of them bent down, picked up something, and waved it triumphantly.

Holmes motioned his minions over and examined the findings. He was talking rapidly now - giving instructions to the troops. I wasn't close enough to make out what was being said, but I thought I heard my name. It was time to leave. I walked briskly back toward the parking lot. As I rounded the corner, I spotted a cop speaking with the booth attendant. I turned and headed instead for the cab stand across the street, grabbed the first one, and told the cabbie to drive around.

After about ten minutes of aimless wandering, I had the taxi drop me at a doughnut shop a few blocks from my office. I went in, but left as soon as I saw the cab drive away, then rounded the corner and ducked into a bar. There was a dark booth at the back, right next to a handy exit. I picked up a copy of the afternoon edition of The Press to hide behind, slid into the booth with my back to the wall, ordered a Scotch, and unfolded the paper. The front page headline shouted, 'Heiress Found Dead at Steel Pier.' I sipped my drink as I absorbed the report.

"**Atlantic City, NJ. Monday, July 23, 1979.-** Tobacco heiress Celine Sutherland was found dead yesterday on the beach by the Steel Pier," I read. "According to local police, the body of the 30-year old sister of the CEO of Sutherland Smokes was half-hidden under the Boardwalk. First reports are that the victim was shot at close range.

"Atlantic City police say they have a suspect, but are not prepared to release a name at this stage in the investigation. A note believed to be from the suspect was found clutched in Sutherland's left hand, according to a source inside the department.

"Sylvia Sutherland broke down when she was informed of her sister's murder, and was placed under sedation. Gordon Sethwick, her husband and the CFO of Sutherland Smokes, Inc., issued the following statement on behalf of the family: 'We are shocked and heartbroken over this senseless killing. Sylvia, Susan and I will put the entire resources of Sutherland Smokes at the disposal of the police to help find and convict Celine's killer.' Susan Sutherland, the youngest of the three sisters, is a graduate student in the Food Science Department at the University of Vermont. She left for Atlantic City as soon as she was informed of her sister's death, and is expected to arrive at the Sutherland family home late tonight. A private interment will be held later this week."

Six

The place was starting to fill up with the Happy Hour crowd. The bartender switched the TV set behind the bar to the local news. I couldn't see the screen from where I was sitting, but it was clear that Celine's murder was the lead story. When I heard the voice of Lt. Holmes informing the reporter that an arrest was imminent, I decided that it was time to go. I refolded the paper, tucked it under my arm, and walked briskly to the office, where I found Millie, sitting distraught and disheveled on the floor, surrounded by manila file folders that were spilling their contents onto the carpet. "Dick!" she exclaimed, her words tripping over each other in their haste to leave her mouth. "There you are. The cops came back with a search warrant. They went through all the files. Everything is everywhere!"

"Slow down, Millie," I said, as I helped her to her feet. "What did they take with them?"

She paused for a mental inventory, then ticked off the items on the fingers of her left hand as she went through the list. "They took everything on the top of your desk," she said. "All the notes, the mail - including the bills - your calendar pad, everything. They emptied both wastebaskets. They took the ribbon cartridge out of my typewriter. They went through the file cabinet, looking at stuff, but I don't think they took any of it. Just left it all in a big pile on the floor." She hesitated. "And they took the files from your locked desk drawer."

Millie could see that the last item staggered me, and added quickly. "They asked me to unlock the drawer, but I told them that you were the only one who had a key to your desk. Then one of the cops asked me what was in the drawer. I told them that I didn't know. They threatened to arrest me for interfering with the search, but then they just broke the lock and took everything."

I thought for a moment about the contents of the locked desk drawer, which had contained all of the notes and documents pertaining to Celine and to Sutherland Smokes. It was fortunate that I'd entrusted Celine's original package to the United States Postal Service; by now, it should be in safe hands. "It's OK, kid," I reassured Millie, who looked to be on the verge of tears. "Everything's gonna be OK."

"Dick, what's wrong?" Millie furrowed her brow. "Did I screw up? I tried calling you over and over, but you didn't pick up."

"Millie, you did just fine," I reassured her. "Look, there are some things I have to do. Are you OK?"

"I guess," she nodded. "Dickie, are you in big trouble?"

I placed a finger under her chin and tilted her tear-stained face upwards until I could look directly into her worried blue eyes. "Nothing I can't handle," I assured her. "Look, I want you to go straight home and stay there. If the cops want to talk to you, call Gus. Don't say a word to the cops without him at your side." I opened the Rolodex on Millie's desk and pulled out a card that read 'Julius Augustus, Attorney at Law' followed by a series of phone numbers. "Keep this card with you," I told her. She nodded her understanding. I smiled and chucked her gently on the chin with my fist. "Atta girl. I knew I could count on you." I was rewarded by a wan smile, a fierce hug and a salty kiss. "Here's looking at you, kid," I said, doing my best Bogart impersonation. I tossed her a jaunty half-salute, and left, the taste of Millie's tears lingering on my lips.

I thought about going home, but decided against it. I didn't want to make it too easy for Holmes and his sidekicks to find me. I needed a quiet place to think. My car was still parked in the public lot near the Steel Pier, so I caught a cab and had the driver drop me off at Atlantic and Tennessee, a few blocks from the Imperial Hotel. A 'stone's throw' from the Boardwalk according to its brochures, the Old Lady of Maryland Avenue was the hotel of choice for vacationing upper middle class families prior to the outbreak of World War II. The imposing red brick structure was accented by hexagonal turrets at its four corners and the roof parapets were covered with cornices. Fire escapes zig-zagged down the center front and center back of the building. Above the ground floor, the hotel was set back from the street, allowing for a large loggia that ran across the entire front of the structure. The window frames, the support pillars for the loggia roof, and all of the decorative trim were painted pristine white. Guests resided in the main building; their body servants slept and took their meals in a sand-brown brick hotel annex located next door at the corner of Maryland and Pacific. A narrow lane with the grand name of South States Avenue ran behind both buildings and provided access for service vehicles.

The Imperial began a gradual downhill slide after the war. Wealthier families were attracted to the newer Atlantic City hotels right on the Boardwalk, or flew off to warmer beach destinations in the Carolinas and Florida, while the less well off only could afford short stays. In November 1963, a fire destroyed the annex and damaged the main structure. The owners patched up the damage to the hotel and soldiered on. But the Imperial never recovered its former glory or its clientele. These days, most rooms rent by the hour. An overnight guest is considered long-term. And a customer who books a room for a week is a celebrity. My room - held on permanent reserve for me under an assumed name in exchange for past and future services rendered - is on the top floor of the hotel near the rear fire exit.

I walked into the lobby and looked around. It was empty, except for a piano player who was hammering out the notes of the Imperial Waltz, an uninspired tune written by an accordion player who spent a summer at the

Imperial a year or two before the fire, and who endowed the owner with the non-existent royalties in lieu of paying his bill. The sofas and armchairs, upholstered in red velvet worn smooth from decades of hosting a variety of bottoms, were unoccupied. I took in the red and gold wallpaper - the height of elegance in the '40s - with its residual scorch marks and water stains from the '63 fire, the dusty, half-lit chandelier and the once-red plush carpet, then followed the threadbare path in the carpet that led from the front entrance to the registration desk. "Any messages for me?" I asked Joey, the desk clerk.

"Nothing, Mr. Trotwood," he told me. "Here's your room key."

I thanked Joey and went up to my room, where I keep a few changes of clothes and an emergency stash of greenbacks. I called Gus to tell him what had happened, then stretched out on top of the bed and put my brain into neutral. When I opened my eyes, the sun was streaming through the east-facing window. As I sat up, I heard an insistent knocking at the door. "Open up," a familiar voice rapped out. "Police. Open up."

I stumbled to the door and opened it, to be greeted by Lt. Holmes. "Damien Dickens," he announced, "you are under arrest for the murder of Celine Sutherland."

Holmes strode past me into the room, followed by Sgt. Sherlock. "How did you find me?" I asked, wondering how I had managed to screw up.

"Good old fashioned police legwork." Holmes smiled, allowing his satisfaction to show. "We found your car in the Steel Pier lot (it's impounded by the way). We looked for you at your apartment first, of course, then tried your office. We visited your secretary's apartment, but she claimed not to know where you were. So we started canvassing, showing your picture at all the hotels and dives in town. We covered the car rental agencies, the bus station, the train station and the airport, too. Put enough pairs of feet on the job and it gets done quickly."

"Alright, Dickens," growled Sgt. Sherlock, clearly savoring the moment. "You know the drill. Hands against the wall and spread those legs." He pushed me none too gently against the nearest wall, frisked me thoroughly, turned me around, and cuffed my wrists in front of me. "Let's go," he said, shoving me toward the door.

"Aren't you forgetting something?" I asked. "Isn't there something you're supposed to tell me? Something that's written on a little card?"

"Go ahead and read him his rights," Holmes jerked his head toward me.

"What's that, Sherlock?" I asked. "When did you learn how to read?"

"Shut up, Dickens," Sherlock muttered, fumbling in his pockets for the Miranda card.

"Here, use mine." Holmes extracted a card from his wallet and handed it to the sergeant. Sherlock squinted at the words as though he had never seen them before. "OK, Dickens," he took a deep breath. "You have the right to remain silent. Anything you say can and will be used against you in a court of law. You have the right to speak to an attorney, and to have an attorney present during any questioning. If you cannot afford a lawyer, one will be provided to you at government expense." He exhaled the final words on the Miranda card and turned to Holmes. "Can we go now, Lieutenant?"

"When do I get to call my attorney?" I asked.

Holmes fielded that one. "After you've been processed, Mr. Dickens, as you know very well. Quit stalling."

The three of us squeezed into the hotel's small, decrepit elevator and creaked slowly down to the lobby. A couple of uniformed cops were waiting at the front entrance and held the doors open as our little procession advanced through to the street, accompanied by catcalls and a smattering of ironic applause. I was stuffed into the back seat of a waiting squad car parked right outside the hotel entrance; Sherlock shoehorned himself behind the wheel with Holmes riding shotgun. And we were on our way, the blaring sirens and flashing lights cutting a path through the morning traffic like Moses parting the Red Sea.

Seven

I knew the drill, of course. Before I left the force I had processed my share of perps. But Sherlock took delight in turning the operation into a circus while making a show of avoiding one: the arrival at the loading dock door, ostensibly to avoid the press, who had been so carefully and deniably tipped off, the handcuffs dramatically covered by a draped jacket, the melodramatic hiding of my face behind a sheaf of documents. Inside, things were just as bad. Nearly every cop who wasn't on patrol was hanging around on one excuse or another to witness my booking; the crime reporter for The Press and the local broadcast boys and girls were flitting around like butterflies so that they could sting me like bees on their nightly news reports.

Somehow, I kept my cool through the fingerprinting, the mug shots, the inventory of my pockets, and the line-up. Somehow, I didn't take a swing at the nearest self-proclaimed journalist with his inane 'How do you feel?' Somehow, I made it to the last act of the circus - the interrogation room - with my dignity mostly intact. Sherlock steered me into a chair, removed my handcuffs, and left the room without a word. I swiveled around to survey the windowless space. It was about nine feet by twelve, with a five-foot long wooden table, around which were placed four chairs. I was in a chair that faced what appeared to be a blank wall. I sat there in the silence, staring at the wall, waiting for something - anything - to happen. I lost all track of time; my Casio was in an envelope with the rest of my inventoried possessions, and there was no clock in the room. I knew that there were cameras on me; I knew the mikes were live. I sat quietly, outwardly calm, willing myself to wait for them to show their hand.

Eventually, Holmes entered the room. He read me my rights again - that was part of the drill - to have a taped record for the court. Then he asked if I wanted to make a statement.

"Sure I'll make a statement," I answered. "Here's my statement. I'm stating that I want to call my lawyer. That's my statement."

"He's already on his way over," Holmes replied. "Your secretary heard about your arrest on the radio and called him. But I thought that we could talk while you're waiting for him to arrive. You know, Dickens," he added, "you're in a pretty tight spot."

"That's not how I see it. Think I'll wait for Gus." I folded my hands on the table in front of me, smiled with what I hoped was an air of confidence, and prepared myself for a long wait. Holmes sat a while and watched for a break in my composure, but I wasn't giving away any freebies. Finally, he stood, shrugged, and left the room. By the time I counted to eight, Sherlock barreled his way through the door and into my face.

"You killed Celine Sutherland," he snarled, punching the table top with his right fist. "First you blackmailed her; then, when she told you last Saturday's payment would be her last, you killed her. We can prove it. We found your gun on the beach." He removed my gun from a small tote bag that was in his left hand and slammed it, evidence tag and all, onto the table. "We found a blackmail note on the victim's body," he continued, as he placed a piece of crumpled paper beside the gun. "And we found this when we searched your apartment."

'This' was an emerald-studded evening bag that looked exactly like the empty bag I had left with Benny the pawnbroker. Only now it was bulging - the zipper straining to remain closed. I couldn't help myself. "What's inside the bag?" I asked.

"As if you didn't know!" Sherlock undid the zipper and held the bag open for me to see. "There's ten grand in there," he announced. "Ten grand! You took the bag from her and shot her dead. Now, why not save the county the cost of a long trial. Tell us everything and maybe you'll get off with life-plus-fifty."

I peered inside the bag, and saw an embroidered 'S' in the lining. This was the same evening bag that I had found in my jacket pocket during my dump truck ride. The bag that I had left with Benny for safekeeping. I was shaken; it took all of my concentration and determination to sit silent and still. Someone had gone to a hell of a lot of trouble to frame me, and I needed to figure out who. Above all else, I needed to keep my mouth shut until I could talk to Gus.

Once he saw that I wasn't going to say anything, Sherlock grabbed me by the arm, lifting me out of my chair. "So be it, Dickens. Let's see how you like your new roommates," he growled as he slapped the cuffs back on my wrists and marched me to a holding pen. The guard unlocked the door; Sherlock shoved me inside and slammed the door shut after me. I stuck my hands up against the bars for him to remove my cuffs. Then I watched, my heart pounding, as Sherlock sauntered back down the hall, whistling 'The Imperial Waltz' as he twirled the handcuffs nonchalantly in his right hand.

I turned and looked at my surroundings. The holding pen was about fifteen feet square. Except for the barred cell door, the walls of the room consisted of painted cinder blocks. A toilet and sink were fixed to the wall in a back corner of the cell; an opaque shower curtain on a curved rod provided an illusion of privacy for the user. A single high, barred window, centered on the wall opposite the door, allowed a modicum of light into the cell. Two incandescent ceiling fixtures, protected with stiff wire mesh, supplemented the meagre natural light. The large cell held the usual assortment of drunks, pimps and pickpockets, with a leavening of self-styled toughs. Two of the latter sidled up to me. "Hey, Dickens, waddaya in for?" I didn't bother answering. I walked over to the bench against the wall, insinuated myself between a pair of the least offensive smelling drunks, and sat. The eyes of the other inhabitants of the holding pen pressed down on me. I rested my elbows on my knees and allowed my head to drop into my hands.

I must have remained in that position for an hour or more. It was the sound of my name that caused me to look up into the face of Julius Augustus III, lawyer and friend to all penurious private eyes. I walked to the holding pen door; the guard let me out and escorted us to a nearby interview room. There was nothing remarkable about the room. It was roughly eight feet by ten, windowless - except for the mesh-reinforced glass pane in the door - and painted institutional gray. The floor was finished with black and white linoleum tiles laid in a checkerboard pattern. The room held a plain wooden table and matching chairs; a black wall phone hung to the right of the doorway. I stood and looked at Gus until the door closed behind us. We both heard the 'click' of the automatic lock.

Gus was a small man - no more than five-seven - and carried himself like an athlete. Always a natty dresser, he was wearing charcoal gray trousers, a battleship gray double-breasted blazer, a white button-down shirt, and a school tie. Gus always wore a school tie. He collected them, and matched the tie to the occasion. Today, he was sporting his orange and black Princeton tie, with its classic diagonal stripes. Not that he had ever attended Princeton, mind you. He was a Pepperdine graduate, with a law degree from the Thomas Jefferson School of Law in San Diego. He just liked to wear Ivy League school ties.

Gus opened his briefcase and pulled out a recorder gizmo. "OK Dick," he assured me, as we sat down facing each other, "We can talk freely. This little beauty will cancel out any live mikes in range of our voices. Now let's hear it. What happened?"

"What happened is that I've been set up," I answered angrily. "I didn't kill Celine. I was working for her, for chrissake! Now how soon can you get me out of here?"

"Not that easy," Gus answered, shaking his head. "I've been talking to George Nicholby, the D.A. That's what took me so long. The arraignment is set for tomorrow morning, and he's going to ask that you be held without bail."

"What?" I leapt to my feet. "What kind of crap is that?"

"Calm down, Dick." Gus pushed me back into my chair. "I said he was going to ask for that. I don't think he'll succeed. But the judge might set a pretty tall bail for you to meet. Can you?"

I shrugged and tilted my chair onto its hind legs as I turned my pockets inside out.

"I get the picture." Gus shook his head ruefully. "Let me work on this. Meanwhile, I need you to fill me in on what happened. Start by telling me everything you know about Celine Sutherland." I sat silently for a minute or two, collecting my thoughts. I could still remember the first time I met Celine. She was a teenager, with a rebellious streak that was as much a part of her as her silky auburn hair.

"Celine insisted on carving out her own path," I began. "She chose to go to Bennington College in Vermont rather than follow her father and her sister to Princeton. She left Bennington in 1970, at the end of her sophomore year, transferring to another school. And not just any school. Not Celine. She insisted on San Diego State University, one of the most notorious party schools in the country, and just an eye blink away from the Mexican border.

"Back then, whatever Celine wanted, she got. She was the first child of Arthur Sutherland's second marriage, and thoroughly spoiled. Arthur's first wife was Lois Olivier Barnstable, the widow of his business partner; he adopted Lois's five-year old daughter, Sylvia, and would have adopted her son, Arnold, too. But Arnold opposed the marriage and refused to have anything to do with Sutherland. 'I have my principles,' he told his mother when she begged him to accept her decision to remarry. However, Arnold's principles did not prevent him from accepting Arthur Sutherland's financial support through college and law school, even as he spurned the Sutherland name.

"Sylvia was eleven when her mother died in childbirth. Arthur Sutherland remarried two years later, and Celine was born when Sylvia was sixteen. A third daughter, Susan, completed the family. Arthur's second wife died a few months after Susan's birth, and the task of raising the two young girls fell to Sylvia, who was far more interested in the Sutherland business interests than in mothering her two step-sisters. Sylvia hired a nanny to care for the girls, and immersed herself in the intricacies of Sutherland Smokes. As Celine grew into her teens, she distanced herself from her father and Sylvia. In college, she channeled most of her considerable energy into having a relentlessly good time. She ran with the fast crowd in San Diego, spending her days surfing and her nights partying. Somehow, she managed to drag a C-minus average into her Senior year. Then she met Paul. Three weeks later, Celine disappeared.

"Arthur wasn't too worried at first; she had gone off before. But when a couple of weeks went by without any word from her, he asked for my help - I had left the police force and was working as a security guard for Sutherland Smokes at the time. I headed out west and poked around until I found Celine in an Ensenada dive - drunk on tequila, high on hash, and turning tricks for Paul. Her money, driver's license, and passport were long gone. I managed to spirit her away by pretending to be a john, and we slipped quietly across the border, mingling with a group of migrant farm workers for camouflage. Arthur had a private jet waiting for us at Gillespie Field in San

Diego, and I delivered his protesting prodigal daughter back home."

I paused in my narrative; Gus laid down his pen and held my gaze. "Then what happened" he asked.

I sighed, then resumed. "About a month later, Arthur suffered his third, and final, heart attack. Arthur's death changed something in Celine. She checked herself into the Egg Harbor Health Sanatorium for six months to kick the booze and drugs, enrolled at Princeton to complete her BA, then breezed through Harvard's MBA program in record time. She worked for a Trenton, NJ management consultant for a few years until, at 28, she declared herself ready to join Sutherland Smokes." I paused, then added, "Arthur Sutherland paid me a generous bonus for bringing Celine home - enough to allow me to start my own detective agency. But I had no further contact with the family after rescuing Celine, and was happy to keep it that way."

"And there was nothing else between you and Celine?"

I looked at him, not quite sure where he was going. "What are you trying to get at, Gus?"

"Rumor has it that you and Celine had an affair back then." Gus looked distinctly uncomfortable, his eyes shifting down to his notepad, then focussing on the wall behind me. "That you seduced her," he added.

"Since when have you started listening to rumors, Gus?" I strained to keep myself under control. My fists clenched involuntarily and my voice dropped to an intense whisper. "There was absolutely nothing between Celine and me." I chewed and spat out each individual word. "Nothing. She was a teenager in trouble, for chrissake, and I was being paid to rescue her." I stopped and struggled to regain control of my temper. "Someone is trying to smear me, Gus," I added. "Probably the same person who set me up as the fall guy for Celine's murder."

Gus held up his hand, then let it fall. "I believe you, Dick," he said. "But I had to ask." I grunted an acknowledgment, and he prompted me to continue.

"The next time I saw Celine," I said, "was Monday of last week. July 16th." I walked him through the sequence of events, starting from when Celine hired me and ending with my arrest. I told him about the visits from Sylvia Sutherland and Gordon Sethwick, and the strange business with the emerald bag and the green pearl earring. I told him about my visit to Benny's pawn shop. Gus gave me an odd look at that, but said nothing. He just let me ramble on. When I finally finished my story, he asked, "Is that everything, Dick?"

I thought for a moment, then lowered my voice to a whisper. "Did you receive the registered mail that I sent you? That large brown envelope marked Confidential?"

He nodded. "It was delivered last Friday."

"What did you do with it?"

"It's in my wall safe."

"Did you open it?"

"No. I wanted to talk to you first." Gus leaned back and gave me a hard stare. "What's this about, Dick?"

I shook my head. "Not now, Gus. Not here." I looked at him, my eyes and voice pleading. "Gus, half of the hoods in that holding pen would like nothing better than to throttle me in my sleep. You have to get me out of here."

He nodded and patted me on the shoulder. "I'll do the best I can for you, Dick," he said. "You know I'll do my best." He gathered up his recording gizmo, replaced it carefully in his briefcase and walked out of the room, leaving me alone with my thoughts.

Eight

After a while, a guard came to escort me to my new home. The private holding cell was eight feet square, and boasted a cot that looked older than I was - equipped with a mattress to match - a flush toilet that had neither a lid nor a seat, and a small sink with cold and cold running water. I looked askance at the mattress, with its abstract pattern of stains of unknown (though likely biological) origin, and decided that I'd spend the night on the painted concrete floor. Even so, I was grateful to be out of the communal holding pen. At least I wouldn't have to watch my back.

I was awakened the following morning by the sound of a guard shoving a bundle through the bars of my cell. I opened the package and found my electric shaver, some toiletries and a change of clothes. I washed as best I could, shaved, and dressed for my arraignment. I had no appetite for breakfast when it arrived, but managed to choke down a cup of coffee. By the time the guard returned to conduct me to court, I was looking almost human, and felt nearly as good as I looked.

Entering the courtroom was like stepping onto the set of a Perry Mason episode. The judge's bench was on a raised dais, with the witness box attached to its left side at a slightly lower elevation. An empty jury box with twelve minimally upholstered chairs stood against the wall to the left of the witness box and at a 90° angle to the dais. Facing the bench were two long tables, separated from each other by about six feet of clear space; George Nicholby, the D.A., was already in his seat at the table nearest to the jury box, making a show of studying the contents of a file folder. Gus was standing at the other table, removing files from his briefcase. Behind the tables, a waist-high railing separated the actors from the audience. The spectators' gallery was furnished with pews that could accommodate up to two hundred people, and was about half full. I

49

spotted Millie in the front row of seats, directly behind Gus. She waved, and smiled wanly; I managed to smile back at her. The Sutherland family was installed across the aisle, behind the District Attorney. Sylvia Sutherland was draped in stylish mourning. She wore a chic, black bolero jacket over a black dress; a black pillbox hat - the kind that Jackie Kennedy made popular back in the '60s - was perched on her head. Her jewelry was restricted to a short string of jet black pearls, and matching black pearl earrings. She held a black lace handkerchief in her left hand, and touched it delicately to the corners of her eyes whenever she saw someone look her way. Gordon Sethwick, seated to the right of his wife, was dressed in a charcoal-gray suit with a white shirt and black necktie; his cuff links and tie tack were adorned with solitary jet black pearls. As I watched, Sethwick danced obsequious attendance to his wife's show of distress, gently patting her arm whenever she touched her hanky to her perfectly made-up eyes. On Sylvia's left was a young woman, also entirely in black, except for her eyes, which were bloodshot and red-rimmed. This must be Susan, the kid sister, I figured. Not such a kid, either, I noticed. Completing the tableau to Susan's left was Arnold Barnstable, the family attorney.

I turned my full attention to Gus. Today, he was wearing his 'dress to impress' outfit; a three-piece charcoal-grey suit, a white shirt with French cuffs, and a crimson necktie emblazoned with a single gold Harvard shield. His cufflinks were gold - gold-plated, anyway - and his vest was adorned with a gold fob watch and chain. He waited for me to be escorted to the table, shook my hand, and motioned me to a seat. I paused to greet Millie, who leaned over the rail to give me a hug of encouragement, before sliding into my chair. "I've got bad news, Dick," Gus began. "I've been talking to Nicholby again, and to the judge. They're treating you as a flight risk. I managed to get them to agree to bail, but it's a steep one. Nicholby's going to ask for a half million. Cash."

"But that's impossible," I sputtered. "No way I can raise that kind of money. And where do they get this 'flight risk' crap?"

"The D.A.'s office is getting pressure from the Sutherland family and their connections. Nicholby will point to your having been arrested while registered in a hotel under an assumed name after abandoning your car in a public lot. I'll try to argue it again," he added, "but the judge will go along with Nicholby on this. Judge Hawthorne is up for reelection this fall, and the Sutherlands are his biggest backers." I was about to protest again, but Gus placed a warning finger to his lips, then pointed at an open door next to the judge's dais. A bailiff entered the room, announcing the obligatory, "All rise." As everyone stood in response, Judge Hawthorne strode into the courtroom and ascended to his bench. He was of short stature, perhaps 5'7", with a ruddy complexion and a full head of steel gray hair. His black robes and horn-rimmed spectacles added dignity and authority to his otherwise ordinary appearance. He stood facing the room, peering first at the Sutherland family, then at me, then back to the Sutherlands and, finally, nodded to the District Attorney before motioning everyone to sit.

Everything went down just as Gus said it would. The D.A. brandished my gun and the blackmail note in front of the judge. Gus objected strenuously to the theatrics, but to no avail. Judge Hawthorne ordered me bound over for trial, and set my bail at half a million. Cash. As I was led out of the courtroom, I looked over my shoulder just in time to see a brief smirk of satisfaction cross Sylvia's face, as a stricken Millie fled the room.

So, there I was again, sitting on the stained mattress on the rusty cot in my 8 x 8 cell, forearms on my thighs, shoulders hunched, and head drooping. I declined lunch when the cart made its rounds. Dinner likewise. What was the use? I spent the night sitting and brooding. Celine was dead and it was my fault. I had failed her. I deserved to be stuck in this hole, even though I hadn't pulled the trigger. The following morning, I was still deep in a brown study - so deep that I didn't hear the footsteps, the turn of a key in the lock, or the metallic sound of the cell door sliding open.

"Get up, Dickens." I stood so abruptly that Sherlock had to jump back in order to prevent his chin from colliding with the top of my head. "You've made bail," he muttered, clearly unhappy at the news. "Come with me."

I followed him like an automaton, wondering if this was a trick to squeeze a confession out of me. But there was Gus, hand held out to shake mine. "You're out, Dick," he said. "Get processed, go home, and catch your breath. Come to my office at two o'clock and we'll talk."

"Where's Millie?" I asked.

"She's getting your car out of the pound. She'll park it at your office."

"Is she OK? She looked pretty upset yesterday in court."

"She's OK, Dick."

"Are you sure?" I pressed him. "Is there something you're not telling me?"

"Later, Dick," was all I could get out of him. "We can talk about it later."

I wanted to ask Gus who had put up my bail, but I wasn't sure I'd like the answer. And I figured Gus wouldn't tell me, anyway. Not here. Not in front of Sherlock. Gus gave me a last half-salute and left me to be processed out. Thirty minutes later, I was a free man. My P.I. license was suspended, my gun permit was suspended, and I was admonished not to leave the state without permission. But I was free, whatever that meant.

I grabbed a cab and went home. The place was a wreck, thanks to the cops. I found the phone under a pile of sofa cushions and called Millie's apartment. She didn't answer. I left a message on her machine, then tried the office. No joy. A few minutes later, I made the phone rounds again. Still nothing. I called Gus. "I'm home," I told him. "I can't reach Millie. I'm worried about her. Is she OK?"

"Stop worrying about Millie, Dick," he replied. "She's a big girl; she can take care of herself. You just get yourself cleaned up, then get your sorry ass downtown."

Bowing to the inevitable, I showered, shaved, dressed, and took a cab to my office. It was locked. I fished the key out of my pocket and went inside. Someone - Millie, no doubt - had started to tidy up the chaos that the cops had left in the wake of their search; stacks of bulging manila file folders covered the tops of both desks and the seats of every chair. I shifted a stack of folders, sat down at my desk, and stared at the phone. 'Millie, where are you?' I wondered. 'Why is Gus dodging my questions?' Well, there was only one way to find out. I pushed myself to my feet, locked up, and walked over to the Law Offices of Julius Augustus III, across the street and just one block away.

Gus's office, on the third floor of the Garden State Building at 1125 Atlantic Avenue, was larger than life, like its proprietor. The outer office was decorated with Stickley furniture: a solid oak reception desk, a small sofa and side chair, and a matching coffee table. This was the domain of Barbara Carruthers, legal secretary extraordinaire. She stood when I entered, a smile of sympathy on her face. "He's waiting for you, Dick," she said. "Go right in." I walked into Gus's private office. His 'Inner Sanctum' he called it. The Stickley executive cherry-wood desk was the centerpiece of the room; a matching set of glass-front book cases, replete with law books and journals, lined one wall. A connecting door led from Gus's private office into a small adjoining conference room. Gus was seated behind his desk in a leather swivel chair, glowering at the contents of a file. Two straight backed armchairs with leather-upholstered seats sat side by side facing the desk.

"What kept you?" Gus growled as I slid into one of the armchairs. Everyone seemed to be growling at me these days.

"I stopped by the office on my way over. I thought I might find Millie there." He raised a quizzical eyebrow at me. "I'm worried about her, Gus. She ran out of the courtroom yesterday in tears, and I haven't seen or spoken to her since."

"Millie asked me to give you a message." Gus shifted in his chair and stared down at his desk blotter, unable to meet my gaze. "She said that you should meet her at Happy's at 5:30. She needs to talk to you."

"Why all the mystery? Do you know what this is about?"

"She wants to tell you herself," Gus said, clearly uncomfortable with his role as go-between. "Now, let's deal with your situation."

"No, not quite yet," I said. "First, tell me who I'm into for the half-million cash bail."

"Jocko. Didn't you read what you were signing? Jocko put up the bail."

"Yes, I read it," I retorted. "But Jocko doesn't have four bits to rub together, let alone a half-million in cash. Who's he fronting for?"

"For me." I rose abruptly, turning as I did so in the direction of the soft female voice. And found myself staring into the determined young face of Susan Sutherland.

Stunned, I could manage only the single word, "Why?"

"Because I don't believe you murdered my sister," she replied. "And I need your help to find her killer."

Well, the last thing I wanted was to get mixed up with yet another Sutherland sister. But, what the hell? It's not like I had any better options. "OK," I said, "let's talk."

I glanced over at Gus, raised an eyebrow and cocked my head. He took the hint. "Why not use my conference room?" he suggested, gesturing in the direction of the connecting door. "I'll be here at my desk if you need me."

I led Susan into the conference room, held out a chair for her to sit, then walked around to the other side of the table and sat across from her. Looking at Susan was like gazing at a younger version of Celine - a Celine untouched by scandal or betrayal. I started to speak, but my voice caught in my throat. I coughed and began again. "I'm sorry you've lost your sister," I said, choosing my words carefully. "Sorry beyond measure at how she died." Susan bowed her head briefly in silent acknowledgment. "You realize, Susan," I went on, "that I can't work for you as a Private Investigator while my license is suspended."

Susan nodded. "Yes, I understand that. Mr. Augustus explained the situation to me. He also said that you were able to investigate on your own behalf. To clear your name, I mean." She smiled fleetingly. It wasn't a smiling moment. "It would have been difficult for you to do that while locked in a jail cell."

"True enough. Okay." I took a breath, held it a moment, then exhaled with an audible sigh. "Here's how we'll do it. While I'm working on my own behalf, there's no law that prevents me from sharing my results with you. Friend to friend, as it were."

"I was hoping you'd say that." Susan leaned towards me, her clasped hands resting on the table in front of her. "When do we start?"

We spent the next hour exchanging information. I told her what little I knew; she filled me in on her last visit from Celine. When we were done, I had one final question that I needed to ask. "Susan," I said, "why are you so sure I'm innocent?"

She smiled. "I wasn't, at first. Celine told me last week that she trusted you, but I couldn't really be certain until we spoke face to face."

"So, what would you have done if I hadn't met with your approval?"

"I would have withdrawn the half-million bail money," she said with a wink. "And you would have been back behind bars in an instant." She turned serious. "I want my sister's killer found and brought to justice, Mr. Dickens. You must find out who murdered Celine. I'll help you any way I can."

I looked into her eyes and held her gaze. "I'll do my best, Susan," I told her. "I'll do my best," I repeated, as I escorted her out of the conference room and took my leave.

Nine

I left Susan with Gus and headed over to Happy's, checking my watch as I walked in. It was 5:30 on the dot. I looked around for Millie, but I didn't see her at first. As I scanned the room again, I spotted her in a booth in the back corner. Her head was bowed over a coffee cup.

"Hey, kid." I tried for a light tone. "What's that bug doing in your coffee? The backstroke?"

She looked up into my eyes, then back down, staring at her coffee cup. "Hi, Dick," she whispered. I could tell she'd been crying - even without the wadded-up tissue clenched in her left hand.

"What's wrong?" I asked.

"What's wrong?" she repeated. "What's wrong? Do you have to ask?"

"Hey, kid," I said. "We've been through tough times before and everything worked out."

"Not this time, Dick." She shook her head. "Not like this. I'm behind on my rent, my phone's about to be cut off, and I have $56 dollars in the bank. I can't do this anymore."

"Can't do what?"

"I can't live my life not knowing whether you're alive or dead, free or in jail, flush or broke. I can't live from hand to mouth. I need to think of myself for a change." She looked up at me. "I'm quitting, Dick," she said. "I need a regular job with regular hours and regular pay, working for a regular boss. I'm tired of dodging bills, lying to the landlord, and playing cops and robbers. I'm not your 'kid' anymore, Dick."

"But what will you do, Millie?" I asked. "Where will you go?"

"If you think I can't get another job, you're sadly mistaken," she bridled. This was a Millie I'd never seen before - resolute, even a little defiant. "If I could keep your office afloat all these years, I can do anything. I've signed on with the Garden State Agency. I have an interview tomorrow."

"The Garden State Agency? Don't they do the hiring for Sutherland Smokes?"

"That's right, Dick. I have a 9 o'clock appointment with Gordon Sethwick."

I tried to keep my voice and my temper under control. "You're seeing Sethwick? You're going to work for them? After what he and his precious Sylvia have done to me?" As I stood, my indignation overcoming my better judgment, the waiter came over. "Nothing for me, pal," I snarled. "I lost my appetite when I realized that there was a knife sticking out of my back."

"You don't understand, Dick," Millie started to say. I cut her off. "You're wrong. I understand too well. I hope you and Sethwick have a good laugh at my expense." I tossed a handful of coins on the table. "The hemlock is on me," I spat out. "Here's looking at you kid - for the last time." I turned on my heel and barreled my way past an incoming party of six. I didn't want Millie to see the tears that were threatening to spill out of my eyes and down my cheeks.

I stumbled out of Happy's and started walking. I was beyond caring about where I was going. All I could think about was that I had lost Millie. After an hour of purposeless prowling through Atlantic City side streets, I decided to go back to the office. I climbed the stairs and was reaching for my key when I realized that the door was slightly ajar. The room was dark, but I could just make out the shape of someone sitting at Millie's desk. I flung the door open and snapped on the lights. And there was

Millie, half-hidden by stacks of files. She looked up, startled.

"To what do I owe this intrusion?" I asked.

She hesitated, then told me that she had stopped by to drop off her office key and the keys to my car. "Once I was here," she added, waving at the stacks on her desk, "I decided that I should make sure the files were all in order."

I told her not to bother. "Just leave the keys and go," I snapped, my voice cold and clipped. "I don't want you here."

"I'm sorry, Dick," she said, and handed me her keys on the way out.

I sat down at the desk she had just vacated and stared blindly at the stacks of files. After a while, I reached into my pocket for a tissue, and my hand closed on a small piece of cardboard. It was the pawn ticket that Benny had given me in exchange for the evening bag. Suddenly, I remembered the queer look Gus threw at me when I mentioned my visit to Benny. I leaped to my feet. It was time for me to be a detective again. I needed to talk to Benny. I might not have a license anymore, but I had a damned important client. Me!

Fifteen minutes later, I was standing outside Benny's, staring at a patchwork of plywood planks where the plate glass window used to be. I tried the door, which opened to my gentle shove without triggering the bell that usually alerted Benny to the presence of someone in the store. Something else about the pawn shop had changed, too. Instead of Benny behind the counter, I was face to face with a stranger - a twenty-something macho kid dressed in black leather pants and a matching biker's vest that dangled open to reveal a once-white T-shirt.

"Who are you?" I asked.

"Bruno," he grunted. "Waddaya want, Pop?"

"I need to talk to Benny."

"He ain't here."

"Where is he?"

"Who wants to know?"

I paused the game of verbal Pong to take a closer look at Bruno. He was tall - probably 6'1" or so - and sported a short, purple-dyed Mohawk that was centered between a pair of lightning-bolt tattoos peeking through the stubble on his newly shaved scalp. His face, ears and tongue displayed a variety of studs and rings. The lightning-bolt motif was replicated on his bare arms and on the back of both hands, which rested, palms down and fingers splayed, on the counter top.

"I asked you a question, Pop," he reminded me. "Are you deaf, or just dumb?

"My name is Dickens," I told him. I didn't let on, but something about him was tickling at the back of my brain. "I have business with Benny."

"Uncle Benny is taking a few days off. There was a break-in here a coupl'a nights ago, and he was pretty shook up. I'm watching the store for him."

"Was he hurt?" I asked.

"Nah, not really. But he was tied and gagged by the thieves. It was a few hours before someone found him."

"What was stolen?"

"I dunno," he shrugged.

"Do you know where he went? Or is he just resting at home?"

"I dunno." Bruno wasn't exactly a fount of knowledge. "He's not home, though."

"Are you sure?"

"'Course I'm sure. He lives at the back of the shop, Pop. Now, what didja wanna see Benny about?"

"I have to pick up something that Benny was holding for me."

"Well, why didn' ya say so, Pop? I can help you with that. Do ya got a stub?"

"A stub?"

"You know, a stub. A ticket," he said impatiently. "Do ya got the pawn ticket stub?"

I fished the ticket out of my pocket and handed it to Bruno. He peered at it for so long that I was beginning to wonder whether he knew how to read. Then he retrieved a ledger from behind the counter, and ran his finger down a few pages. He looked up at me when he reached the halfway point of the fourth page. "Found it," he announced.

Bruno walked over to the boarded-up display window, reached in, and withdrew the silver French horn from its place of honor. "Here's your horn," he said, handing it to me. "That'll be fifty bucks."

"That's not right," I said. "He was holding a green evening bag for me. With doodads on it."

"We ain't got nothin' like that, Pop." There was that annoying shrug again.

"Then give me back the stub. I'll wait until Benny's back." I held out my hand.

"Suit yourself, Pop." He delivered one last shrug as he placed the ticket stub in my hand. I turned to leave the shop, and could feel his eyes following me out the door. I stood on the sidewalk for a couple of minutes, staring at the door to the shop before deciding to head home. It had been a long day.

Ten

I must have been more tired than I thought. I fell onto my bed without bothering to take off my shoes and was asleep before you could say 'Sutherland Smokes.' I dreamed that I was the target in a carnival midway game. People were throwing green baseballs at me, trying to knock me off my perch. Every time someone hit the target, a bell would clang, and I would drop into a tub of water. I woke in a cold sweat to the sound of my telephone ringing. It was Gus. We agreed to meet in his office at nine o'clock to 'go over my situation,' as he put it.

I staggered into the shower and turned the water on full-force. The initial cascade of cold water cleared my head, and I could feel the neurons inside my brain starting to fire up. The first order of business was to track Benny down. Once I had dried off, I fished my little black book out of the night table drawer and thumbed through it. When I got to the R's, I picked up the phone and dialed. The call was answered on the third ring.

"Parole office, Roberts here."

"Hello, Burt," I said. "It's been a while."

"Dickens?" I could hear the surprise in his voice. "I thought you were in jail."

"I'm out." I crossed my fingers before continuing. "Burt, I need a favor."

There was a long pause, then a grudging, "Alright, but not over the phone. Can we meet tomorrow?"

I would have liked it sooner, but I've learned to take what I can get. "OK. Tomorrow. Happy's. Five-thirty." I hung up the phone and looked down at my hand. While I was talking to Burt, I had picked up a pencil and had filled a page of my little black book with lightning bolt doodles. I knew that my right brain had a piece of information that it was trying to send to my left brain, but the left side wasn't ready to receive it yet. I put the address book back in its drawer, dressed, and left my apartment.

I dropped into my office before going to see Gus. To clear my desk, I told myself. I could hear the phone ringing as I fumbled with my keys to the door. I was going to need an answering machine now that Millie was gone. The lock resisted my first attempt to open it, but I reached the phone on the tenth ring. "Dickens," I panted.

"Good morning." The voice at the other end was far too cheerful for my liking. "Is this the Dickens Detective Agency?"

"Yeah, can I help you?" I didn't really feel helpful just then, but the routine reply popped out of my mouth.

"This is Mary Sue Thorpe from the Human Resources office at Sutherland Smokes," the voice chirped. "Am I speaking to Mr. Damien Dickens?"

I knew what was coming next, and I didn't like it. "Yeah, this is Dickens," I grunted.

"Mr. Dickens." Ms. Thorpe was now all business. "We are considering hiring Ms. Millicent Hewitt, and are checking her references. Can you confirm that she was an employee of yours?"

"Yeah." I was determined to say as little as possible, but this nosy broad had no intention of letting me off the hook that easily.

"How long did she work for you?"

"Five years, maybe more," I said.

"Would you say she was a good employee, Mr. Dickens?" I hesitated, remembering the day Millie first walked into my office. Remembering yesterday, when she walked out of it for the last time. I could torpedo Millie's application in just a few words. Then honesty got the better of me. "She was better than good," I admitted. "She was the best." I hung up abruptly.

I thumbed through the stacks of mail that Millie - tidy and thoughtful even while stabbing me in the back - had placed on my desk. It was mostly junk, seasoned with a dunning notice or two. I tossed the junk automatically as I went through the stack, and was just about to sort through the bills when I heard a metallic click from the outer office. I looked up in time to see a white envelope land on the floor below the mail slot. I ran to the door, opened it, and looked both ways down the hall, but I was too late. There was no one in sight. I could hear the faint sound of feet descending the staircase, then a bang as the rear door to the building swung shut. I bent down and retrieved the envelope. It had no return address and no postage, and was simply addressed 'Damien Dickens. Confidential.' I undid the flap and extracted a single sheet of paper. The message, pencilled in block letters, read, 'I need your help. Meet me behind the Imperial Hotel on Friday at midnight.' It was signed 'B.C.' I shoved the note into my jacket pocket and checked my watch. I was late for my appointment with Gus.

Eleven

I covered the block to Gus's office at a brisk jog, jaywalking across Atlantic Avenue against a red light. I was a half-hour late for our 9:00am meeting. I tried to blame my tardiness on the time spent talking to the Thorpe dame from Sutherland's, but Gus wasn't buying it. "Sit down, Damien," was all he said, after listening to my alibi. I knew he was pissed off at me. He only calls me 'Damien' when he's angry. I sat.

"While you've been moping around feeling sorry for yourself," he began.

"I have not been moping." I leaped to my feet, voice raised, and face as red as the rust on my '71 Celica.

"I said, 'Sit DOWN, Damien.' It's not enough that you kept me waiting. You also had Susan Sutherland cooling her heels for half an hour. She dropped in to say good-bye before driving back to Vermont." Gus took a deep breath and continued more calmly. "Look, Dick, you are the best Private Investigator I've ever worked with. But you're behaving like a lovesick teenager. Millie's gone. Get over it." He paused and looked me square in the eyes. "Unless you pull yourself together and start working with me, you're going to find yourself wearing striped pajamas for the rest of your miserable life."

I swallowed hard and nodded. He was right.

"While you've been sitting around with your thumb in your bum," he continued, waving me back into my seat as I half rose in protest, "I've been squeezing some cooperation out of the D.A.'s office. Nicholby instructed the cops to expedite the release to us of copies of their investigation reports. I've already started going through the material." Gus paused. I could tell that he wasn't sure how to phrase the next question. "Dick, what do you know about Celine's son?"

67

I hesitated, trying to decide how much to say, but Gus jumped right in. "I'm your attorney, Dick. I can't help you if you don't tell me what you know."

I had to admit that he was right. "OK, Gus," I conceded. "I learned about him in '72, when I rescued Celine in Tijuana."

"Is that when you first met Celine?"

"Yeah," I nodded. "It was about a year after I left the Atlantic City PD. I was working Security for Sutherland Smokes. When Celine went missing, Arthur Sutherland sent me to find her and bring her home. She told me the story on the flight back from San Diego; she needed to talk to someone, and I was handy. Celine had an affair, and the jerk went and married someone else. A few weeks after his marriage, she discovered that she was pregnant. She decided to adopt the baby out, then tried to put as much distance between her son and herself as she could. That's why she transferred to a school out west. She never told her erstwhile lover about the boy."

"Did she confide in anyone else?"

I shrugged. "Not as far as I know, she didn't. I don't even think that her father knew she was pregnant." I looked up at Gus, who did not appear to be happy with this information.

"No one knew? Sylvia, perhaps, or Susan?" he probed.

I shook my head. "I don't think so. I know that she just told Susan recently. She drove up to Burlington especially for that last week. Why all the questions about the boy, Gus?"

"Because of these." He handed me three sheets of paper. "These are copies, by the way. The police have the originals. The first sheet was found on Celine's body - clutched in her left hand. The other two were retrieved from your office. They were found in the wastebasket next to your desk during the police search."

I stared at the top sheet, which read, 'Bring $10,000 to the Steel Pier tonight at eleven sharp. Come alone. Screw up and your son dies.' The other two were earlier drafts, also typed, but with some minor wording differences and X'd out typing errors. "What are you trying to say, Gus? This is a set up. I didn't send this note." I could hear my voice rising. "What do you take me for?" I was on my feet now, waving the pieces of paper in Gus's face. "These aren't even from my typewriter."

Gus stood, waiting for the storm to subside. "Sit down, Dick," he said in a mild voice as he shoved me gently back into my chair. "How can you be so sure those notes weren't typed on your machine?"

"Because I hate this small lettering - I think Millie calls it 'Elite' - it's too hard to read. Millie tried to get me to go along with it; she said it saved on stationary. But I refused. I got so mad one day that I took the Elite type ball out of the typewriter and threw it out the window. Millie took the hint and only used the larger type face after that."

"What about the drafts that the cops say they found in the trash?"

"They're screwy, too. When I finally had the cash to buy a new typewriter, Millie insisted on the most up-to-date model. She got an IBM Selectric with self-correcting tape. All you do is hit a backspace key, and it erases the mistakes like magic. Even I can make a typed page look perfect the first time. Someone must have planted those papers in the trash to incriminate me."

"Who? When?"

I thought about that for a minute or two, then snapped my fingers. "Could have been Sethwick. He came to the office first thing Monday morning. He insisted on hanging around until I arrived, then started in on me - asking me where Celine had disappeared to. That was before I found out she was dead. I was all stinky from the dumpster and just wanted to get rid of him. He could easily have dropped those sheets in the wastebasket next to my desk."

I held up the copy of the note that had been found on Celine's body. "Do the cops know how this note was delivered?"

Gus leafed through the investigation report before answering. "Apparently, it was given to Celine Saturday evening, during the charity ball. A messenger brought it."

"Did he hand it directly to her?"

"No. It says here that he handed it to Sethwick and asked him to give it to Celine."

I jotted a note to myself. "Gus, I need a copy of the complete investigation file. After I've gone through it, I want to talk to Sethwick and to anyone else who might have seen or spoken with the messenger."

"Good." Gus rang for his secretary. Barbara entered the room, steno pad in hand, spare pencil tucked behind her right ear. She was of moderate height - perhaps 5'6" - with dark brown hair that framed her round face. An air of quiet, dignified efficiency accompanied her into the room. "Barbara, I need a complete copy of this for Dick by the time he's ready to leave." Gus waved his hand at the cardboard file box that was sitting on the floor beside his desk.

"Certainly, Mr. C." Barbara nodded, hefting the box with ease.

I watched her as she left, carefully closing the door behind her. "Gus, there's something I've always wondered." He raised an eyebrow in query. "Why does Barbara call you 'Mr. C'?"

He laughed. "When she first started working for me, she was all business - 'Yes, Mr. Augustus,' 'No Mr. Augustus' - and it drove me crazy. So I told her to call me

'Gus'; but that made her uncomfortable. We compromised; the 'C' stands for 'Caesar' as in Julius Augustus Caesar."

"You know, Gus," I chuckled, "Barbara always reminds me of Della Street. She even kind of looks like Della, don't you think?"

Gus barked a short laugh. "I agree, she does. But please don't tell my wife. Della had a serious case of 'the hots' for Perry Mason." His demeanor grew serious, and he asked "What's your next move, Dick?"

I reached into my pocket, pulled out the sequined bag that I had purchased in the Boardwalk souvenir shop, and tossed it onto Gus's desk. He picked it up, turned it over, undid the zipper, and looked inside. "What's this about, Dick?" he asked.

"It's something else that doesn't fit," I began. "The cops claim that they found Celine's evening bag, with ten grand stuffed inside it, hidden in my apartment, right?"

Gus nodded. "So?"

"So the bag was planted."

"And?"

I stopped a moment to organize my thoughts. "When I woke up in the dump truck, there was a jeweled evening bag in my jacket pocket. I brought it home with me. The jewels looked like emeralds, and the lining felt like silk. There was a monogram in the lining, too."

"That's the bag the cops found in your apartment. I saw it. An uppercase 'S' was embroidered into the lining in silver thread."

"Right. Now, here's the thing. On Monday, before the cops searched my place, I brought the bag to Benny Caravaggio."

"Benny the pawnbroker?" Gus looked puzzled. "Why would you do that?"

"I wanted to know what it was worth. Sylvia was carrying a similar bag when she came to my office the day of the Christmas in July ball. In fact, I thought at the time that it was the same one. But Benny said the bag was worthless - a Boardwalk souvenir. I asked him to hang onto it for safekeeping, and promised him fifty bucks for his trouble. Benny gave me a pawn ticket in case I sent Millie to pick it up."

Gus held up his hand to stop me. "Dick, why would you leave the bag with Benny if he said it was worthless?"

"Because I didn't believe him. It was too well made to be a piece of Boardwalk junk. And it was monogrammed. Also, I had already received a 'courtesy call' from the ACPD - from Sgt. Sherlock and Lt. Holmes, to be precise - and I had a hunch there was something screwy going on. I wanted to keep the bag out of reach of the cops and out of circulation."

"You know," Gus said, "that Benny's place was broken into Monday night?"

"I found that out yesterday, when I went to his shop to reclaim the bag. His nephew, a punk named Bruno, tried to palm a French horn off on me. He said that they 'never had no evening bag.' I took the pawn stub back from him and left."

"So, what's the deal with this bag?" Gus picked it back up and peered inside. "It doesn't look anything like the one the cops found. This piece of crap isn't even lined, much less monogramed, and the so-called emeralds are just plastic sequins."

"Exactly. This bag cost me all of ten bucks. Benny knows his business. There's no way he could have mistaken an emerald-studded bag for this one. I need to find out why Benny told me that the bag I showed him was worthless, and what happened to the bag after I left it with him. My guess is that it was lifted from Benny's shop during the break-in, stuffed with the cash, and planted in my apartment for the cops to find."

"You think that Benny is implicated in this?"

"I don't know what to think. This note was shoved through my office mail slot this morning. I think it's from Benny." I passed the note across the desk to show Gus. "It's signed 'B.C.' He wants to meet me at midnight tonight behind the Imperial."

"Be careful, Dick." Gus wrinkled his forehead, creating a series of parallel worry lines. "I don't want to lose my favorite P.I." He stood and handed me back the note. "I think we've covered enough ground for one session. Grab the files from Barbara on your way out, and check in with me tomorrow. I'll be in the office most of the day."

"Working Saturdays, are you?"

"Yeah." Gus smiled. "You're not my only client, you know."

Twelve

I took my leave of Gus, collecting the box of files from Barbara on my way out. My stomach was telling me that it was lunch time, so I hopped into my car and headed for Petronio's, my favorite pizza take-out. "The usual, Mr. D?" The pimply kid - nephew of the owner, I think - always greeted me the same way. I nodded, and watched as he nimbly tossed the dough and slathered it with tomato sauce. The shredded mozzarella was next, followed by pepperoni slices, sliced fresh mushroom, diced green bell pepper and a smattering of anchovies. Twenty minutes later, I was on my way, steam from the pizza box saturating the interior of my car with essence of melted cheese and soggy cardboard.

I parked the Celica in back and took the stairs. Juggling the pizza and the box of files, I fished for my keys, and unlocked my office door. My desk was just as I had left it - piled high with accumulated mail and file folders that Millie had put there. I cleared some space on the desk with a sweep of my arm, sat down, and dug simultaneously into the police files and the pizza.

I opened the first folder and found myself staring at grainy photocopies of the pictures taken of the crime scene. Celine's body was mostly hidden under the Boardwalk; only her calves and feet were in clear view. Her shoes were lying next to her right hand, as though she had been carrying them while walking on the sand. It looked like her killer may have tried to hide her body under the Boardwalk, but was either interrupted or had run out of steam. There was also a close-up of Celine's left hand, which was curled around a piece of paper - the purported ransom note, no doubt. Photographs and an accompanying diagram documented the widely separated locations on the beach where the cops had found my gun and wallet.

I sat and stared at the images, trying to make sense of them. I was mesmerized by the grainy pictures of Celine. I flashed back to her recent visit to my office, her plea for help. I had failed to protect my client, but I would find her killer. And I would fulfill the rest of my promises to her. My pizza had grown as cold as my appetite. I slammed shut the lid of the pizza box, grabbed the crime scene report, shoved the carton containing the rest of the files under my desk, and locked the office door on my way out. It was time to check out the scene of the crime.

I drove down South Carolina Avenue to the Boardwalk, parked in the public lot and, file folder in hand, crossed over to the beach just south of the Steel Pier. The cops had been all over the area, but I needed to see for myself where Celine's body had lain. The police barriers and crime scene tape were mostly gone; just a stray strip of yellow plastic tape drooped from a post at the edge of the Boardwalk, its tip lying morosely on the sand. It was clear from the parallel rake tracks that the beach maintenance crew had done their job, too. I wasn't expecting miracles.

I consulted the report and located the exact location where Celine's body had been discovered by a pair of teenagers who were looking for a discreet place to study comparative anatomy. According to the report, by the time the cops arrived, any footprints or other marks in the sand had been pretty much messed up by curious onlookers. I crouched down and shone my flashlight under the Boardwalk. The area had been swept in the hunt for the murder weapon, but the beam of light revealed some trash - mostly paper and a few plastic bottles - 'way at the back, blown up against a concrete footing. I crawled under to investigate. Half-buried under a mound of crumpled tissues, old newspapers, sticky condoms, and faded ad flyers for the Steel Pier were two plastic pop bottles that would never again hold liquid. I used a ballpoint pen to fish the pop bottles out from under the rest of the trash. Each one was partially filled with sand and had a neat, round hole punched dead center in its bottom. A .44-caliber hole, it looked like, surrounded by a pattern of crazing in the plastic. I'd read about plastic pop bottles being used to silence a weapon, and these had served that very purpose for somebody. I transferred the bottles into a relatively clean plastic grocery bag that had blown under the Boardwalk, and continued my search. I was about to declare a halt when I noticed a crumpled piece of paper that looked fairly fresh. I flattened it out and shone the light on it. It was a typed note. Heart pounding, I read, 'We have your son. If you want to see him alive again, come at once to the Steel Pier.' There was no signature or any other identifying mark that I could find.

I crawled back out onto the beach, note in hand, and returned to my car. I tossed the bag containing the pop bottles into the trunk, then flattened the crumpled note on the surface of the hood and placed beside it the copy of the ransom note that the cops had retrieved from Celine's hand. Both notes were typed in the same small typeface that I hated - the one Millie always called 'Elite.' As I stared at the two notes, I noticed something else. The upper case 'S' in the word 'Steel' was out of alignment in both notes. Not by much. Not by enough to twig to if you were just looking at a single sheet. But by just enough to suggest that both notes could have been typed on the same machine.

I folded the papers, shoved them in my pocket, and raced back to Gus's office as fast as traffic would allow. "Gus," I said, exploding into his office before he could answer my knock. "I found something. It's another note."

"Give me five minutes, Dick." Gus was on the phone, and looked annoyed at the interruption. I mumbled an apology, and sat down while he finished his call.

"OK, Dick. Now what do you have that's so urgent?"

"I was poking around the crime scene," I explained. "I found this under the Boardwalk, up against a concrete footing." I showed him the note. He read it with a puzzled frown.

"Gus, my hunch is that this is the note the messenger delivered to Celine the night she was murdered. I think the other note was a plant - part of the effort to frame me."

"An interesting theory, but how do you expect to prove it?"

I pulled the copy of the ransom note out of my pocket and put it on Gus's desk. "For starters, look at this." I pointed to the word 'Steel' in both notes. "The 'S' is just a bit wonky. I suspect these notes were typed on the same machine."

Gus pulled a magnifying glass out of his drawer and examined the notes. "Could be," he admitted. "But we'd need to compare the originals to be sure."

"That's what I figured, too. How soon can you arrange that?"

"Let me make a call." Gus reached for his phone and dialed the District Attorney's office. "Uh huh. Monday morning? Can't make it any sooner? OK, I understand. Sure. Thanks." He hung up, frowning. "Sorry, Dick. Not until Monday morning. They're on summer hours."

"Can't be helped, I guess." I stood, gathered up the notes, then thought the better of it. "Can I use your photocopier?" Gus nodded and I ran off a couple of copies of the note I had found. "Here, you'd better hang on to the original." I handed it to him. "I'll see you at the D.A.'s office Monday morning. Nine sharp."

I returned to my office, flipped open the lid to the pizza box, and worked my way simultaneously through the rest of the pizza and the remaining police files. The autopsy and lab reports were in separate folders. According to the pathologist, Celine died from a single bullet to the chest. There was no trace of gunpowder on her clothes or her skin. Except for the entry and exit wounds, Celine's clothing was undamaged - not even a run in her pantyhose. It was unlikely that she had walked any distance in her stocking feet. The lab reports were straightforward - no traces of drugs, toxins or alcohol in her system. A slug found buried in the wood fascia of the Boardwalk was a .44 Magnum - a perfect match to my gun, and the correct calibre for the size of the hole in Celine's chest.

The next file contained statements from various witnesses. Four different people saw a messenger hand an envelope to Gordon Sethwick at the charity ball. I jotted down their names and contact info. Three of the witnesses also saw Sethwick hand the envelope to Celine. I added a mark beside each of their names. I hoped to speak to all four witnesses over the weekend. Also, I made note to contact the organizer of the charity ball to get a complete list of attendees. Others may have seen or overheard something significant, too. The remaining files contained all the miscellanea of the police investigation - results of the searches conducted at my office and my apartment, a list of the evidence collected at the crime scene, activity logs from Holmes and Sherlock, and so forth. I made a series of notes as I worked through the reports and the ice-cold pizza - there were several items that begged for follow-up.

I reached for another slice of pizza, and my hand hit soggy cardboard. I was done. I looked at my watch. Eleven forty-five. I needed to hurry if I was going to make it to the Imperial before midnight. I gathered up all the files, together with my notes, locked up the office and headed for my car, pausing to toss the empty pizza box in a convenient public trash can. The safest place for these files was locked in the trunk of the car, and that's where I put them. I executed a U-turn and headed for the Imperial. As usual, the traffic lights were engaged in a conspiracy against me, and I made it to the hotel parking lot just as the City Hall clock struck midnight. As I was locking the car, a loud series of sharp popping sounds pierced the darkness. There was a brief silence, followed by the scurry of running feet.

I headed for the sounds, which seemed to have originated from the lane behind the hotel. But the footsteps had died away by the time I got there. It was dark as death behind the Imperial - the light over the rear door was out - so I took out my flashlight and shone it around. The area seemed deserted. There was no sign of Benny; he might have been scared off by the shooting, I thought. I figured that I'd better hang around for a while in case he returned. As I stood with my back to the hotel wall, I heard a low-pitched groan to my right. I whipped around and pointed my flashlight in the direction of the sound. The beam picked up something pink and spiky. I lowered the angle of the light slightly, and spotted Bruno, lying crumpled and half-hidden behind a dumpster bin. I ran over and wedged myself in beside him.

"Help," he whispered, clutching my arm. "They shot me. Dickens .... Help ... Benny." I felt his grip on my arm loosen as he passed out.

Thirteen

I eased back out from behind the dumpster, ran to the phone booth on the corner, and called 9-1-1. Then I raced back to Bruno and knelt beside him. He was still out. I felt his pulse. It was weak, but regular. I slapped him on the cheeks to rouse him. "C'mon, Bruno," I begged. "Stay with me."

I saw his eyelids flutter, then open. "Hey, Pop," he whispered.

"Hey, Bruno." I could hear sirens in the distance. The cops and EMTs were coming. There wasn't much time.

"Bruno," I said, my voice an urgent whisper. "Are you the one who sent me the note?"

"Yeah." His voice was very soft, and I bent down until my ear was close to his mouth.

"Why?" He was silent, and seemed to drowse off, so I shook him gently and repeated, "Why, Bruno? Why did you want to meet me here?"

"Because me and Uncle Benny need your help." He paused, his breathing becoming more labored, then went on. "They paid Benny to pull the scam on you with that bag. Then they welched on the rest of the deal. Benny threatened to squeal. Now he's on the run."

"Who, Bruno?" He was going under again. "Stay with me, man. Who paid Benny?" I slapped his cheeks again to rouse him. "Who set me up?" But it was no use.

The sirens were very loud now. I knew that a crowd would be gathering and there would be questions. Questions that I couldn't answer. I headed for my car. And home. I drove slowly, trying to digest what I had learned from Bruno, and wondering what to do next. I needed to find Benny. But first, I needed some sleep.

I've always been able to switch off my brain and fall asleep instantly. But this time my brain wasn't cooperating. I kept thinking about Bruno and Benny. Bruno was dead or dying, and Benny was on the run. In danger. And he was my best link to Celine's murderer. I must have finally fallen asleep, because the next thing I knew, I was being chased down the Boardwalk by lightening bolts launched at me by a bevy of bikers sporting Mohawk haircuts. They all looked like Bruno. The bikers were gaining on me when I was suddenly awakened by a loud ringing in my ears. I sprang out of bed in a cold sweat and scrambled to pick up the phone. It was Gus. "You OK, Dick?" he asked.

I looked at the display on my clock radio. "Geez, Gus. It's just six o'clock."

"I heard about the shooting last night behind the Imperial and wanted to check on you," he explained.

"Yeah, I'm OK."

"You want to tell me about it?"

"Not on the phone, Gus. I'll drop around to your office later this morning." I hung up the receiver, cast a dubious glance at my bed, and decided that I couldn't handle another nightmare. I showered and shaved, which made me feel at least halfway human. Then I fixed myself some toast and instant coffee for breakfast, and thought about my dream. My subconscious had made some connections, and it was now clear to me that Bruno was more deeply implicated in Celine's murder than he had admitted to being. The 'cop' who rousted me on the Boardwalk the night that Celine was killed had lightning bolt tattoos on the backs of his hands. Tattoos just like Bruno's.

I used a last gulp of coffee to wash down my final bite of toast. The toast was stone-cold and the coffee tasted like tepid dishwater. So much for breakfast. I fumbled in a drawer for my phone book, found the home number for Burt Roberts, my contact in the parole office, and picked up the phone. Then I checked my watch and hesitated. Was it too early to call? I didn't want to piss him off.

I dialed the number anyway and held my breath. After about five rings, a sleepy voice grunted what sounded like "Hello?"

"Burt..."

He cut me off. "Dickens, why the hell are you calling me at home? You've got some nerve to ..."

"Burt." I interrupted his tirade. "Do you know Benny Caravaggio?"

"What? Couldn't this wait until our meeting this afternoon?"

"Do you know him, Burt?"

"Yeah." A cautious pause. "I'm his parole officer. Why?"

"I have reason to believe he's in danger. His nephew was shot last night."

"That's a police matter - not a parole office matter. You know that, Dickens. Go talk to the cops and let me get back to sleep."

"I can't go to the cops." I took a deep breath. "This is all tied into the Sutherland killing. I think Benny was involved somehow, but I have no proof. I think he might be able to finger the perp - if we can find him before the killer does."

"When did this become a 'we'?"

"Burt, you owe me!"

There was a long pause. Then a sigh, followed by "What do you need from me?"

I hadn't realized that I was still holding my breath. I started to speak, then had to stop and clear my throat. "I need his contact info, next of kin, any addresses and phone numbers - the usual. The same for his nephew, Bruno Caravaggio, if he's in your system. And it wouldn't hurt if you could give me copies of their records."

"That's all confidential stuff, Dick." Burt was uncomfortable and was starting to hedge.

"Your name won't come into this at all, Burt, I swear. You know I always protect my sources." I paused. "How soon can you have this for me?"

"I'll have to go into the office. How about some time on Monday?"

"How about today?" I knew I was pressing, but Burt was my only lead to Benny. "If you bring the stuff to Happy's, I'll even spring for dinner."

There was another long pause, then he capitulated. "OK, Happy's at six. But you'll have to tell me what's going on before I hand over the information."

"Fair enough. Thanks, Burt. I knew I could count on you." He grunted in reply and hung up. "See you later," I said to the dead air.

I needed to figure out how deeply Bruno and Benny were tied into Celine's murder. I thought about the chain of events that resulted in my leaving the evening bag with Benny. There was no way that the murderer could have known in advance that I would consult Benny. But he or she may have expected - and planned for - me to be curious about the bag, and could have made an advance arrangement with other likely dealers. Especially pawnbrokers. They know how to keep their eyes and hands open and their mouths shut.

I grabbed the Yellow Pages and turned to the P's. The list of pawnbrokers was short. Just two shops - Benny's, and an outfit that called itself Baubles to Bucks. I noted the address of Benny's lone competitor and headed for my car. Driving up the Atlantic Avenue strip, I passed convenience stores, the local Goodwill shop, a few bars, gun shops, and payday loan storefronts. When I reached the 3000 block, I parked, locked the car, and walked the rest of the way.

Baubles to Bucks was located at 3111 Atlantic Avenue, sandwiched between a walk-in chiropractor and a bail bondsman, in a row of shops that were on the street level of a two story brick building. The upper floor was occupied by apartments and offices. There were curtains in some of the upstairs windows, and a couple of them sported air-conditioner units balanced precariously on their sills. One window displayed a small neon sign that featured an illuminated yellow cross and the words "Church of the Blessed Repentance."

The pawnshop sported a faded yellow awning with 'Baubles to Bucks' in mottled gray block letters. Stenciled in yellow paint on the plate glass windows on either side of the door were promises of 'Instant Cash' and 'Discount Loans.' A small plaque above the entry read 'Brian Goodley, Prop.' The door was propped open, and I took that as an invitation to enter. The shop was tidier than Benny's, although the mix of merchandise was about the same. The man behind the counter was tidier, too. He was tall - at least six foot - and slender. His mahogany brown hair was full, and neatly parted on the left; it grew slightly long in back, brushing his collar. He was dressed in a cream-colored shirt, a brown tie with yellow diagonal pinstripes, and a Harris tweed jacket. His eyes, which were the same color as his hair, peered through the lenses of steel-rimmed spectacles. His hands were resting casually on the countertop; his fingernails had been recently manicured and were coated with a clear polish.

"How may I help you?" His deep bass voice, usually incongruous in such a slender man, seemed to fit him.

"Mr. Goodley?" He nodded. "My name is Dickens." I fished a business card out of my pocket and handed it to him. "I'm investigating a shooting."

85

He examined the card carefully, his brow furrowed. "A shooting?"

"Yes. A man was shot last night behind the Imperial Hotel on Maryland. His name was Bruno Caravaggio."

"Benny's nephew?" His eyes narrowed when I mentioned Bruno, and he regarded me warily.

"The same. Do you know Bruno well?"

"Mainly by reputation. I've met him a couple of times," he went on. "He's a petty hood - thinks he's a tough guy. Dresses the part."

"When did you last see him?"

"Hey, you don't think I had anything to do with the shooting, do you?" He thrust his head towards me in emphasis. "I don't remember when I saw him. Maybe a few months ago?" His voice trailed off invitingly.

I reached into my wallet and pulled out a twenty. "Would this help your memory?" He shrugged. I placed a second twenty on top of the first. His eyebrows twitched. I took the last twenty from my wallet and added it to the stack.

"OK," Goodley conceded, slipping the bills into his jacket pocket "he came by the shop a week or two ago." I waited for the punch line. "He was fronting for someone in some kind of scam."

"When exactly was this?"

"It was a couple of days before the 'Christmas in July' charity ball."

"So, what was the scam?"

"Not a scam, exactly," he hedged. "More like a prank."

I raised an eyebrow. "A prank? What kind of prank?"

"Well," Goodley hesitated, then continued in a rush. "Bruno said someone might show up looking to pawn a

86

jeweled evening bag. I was to tell the person that the bag was worthless. It didn't make much sense to me."

"That was it?"

"Pretty much." He shrugged. "But Bruno said that I should try to get the mark to leave the bag with me anyway. I told him he was nuts, but he offered me a hundred dollars, so I humored him."

I knew the answer to the next question, but asked it anyway. "Did the mark ever show?"

"Hasn't yet. But I'm still hoping," Goodley added, "because Bruno promised there would be a grand in it for me if the bag turned up and I held onto it. Guess the deal's dead now that Bruno's been shot."

"It's not just the deal that's dead." I looked Goodley in the eyes, and held his gaze. I wanted to make him sweat before I asked the next question. "Do you have any idea who Bruno was working for?" He shook his head. "Sorry."

I swallowed my disappointment. "You have my card," I reminded him. "If you remember anything else, or if someone contacts you about Bruno or the evening bag, give me a call. My office and home phone numbers are on the card." He mumbled something non-committal in reply. As I left the shop and turned right to walk back to my car, I saw him tear my card in two and drop the pieces into a wastebasket.

Fourteen

I walked back to the car, intending to head over to Gus's office to bring him up to date. I climbed in, started the motor and tuned the radio to WMID just in time to catch, "...severely wounded in a shooting behind the Imperial Hotel last night. A hospital spokesman reports that the shooting victim is in critical but stable condition. The victim's name will not be released until his next-of-kin can be located and notified." I snapped off the radio. Bruno was alive!

I stopped in at a doughnut shop and picked up a mixed dozen to celebrate. Gus and I demolished most of them over coffee as I brought him up to speed. He promised to keep tabs on Bruno's status for me while I worked to track Benny down. I grabbed a last doughnut for the road, and bit into it as I walked back to my car. The chocolate glaze was sprinkled with chopped nuts - and shells, as it turned out. As I started to chew, I heard an ominous cracking sound and felt a stab of pain that radiated up from my jaw into the area under my left eye. I probed the left side of my mouth with my tongue, and discovered a nasty raw, jagged edge where one would expect a smooth enamel surface. I had cracked a tooth.

Cursing with unprecedented fluency, I went back up to Gus's office and called my dentist. I was in luck. He had just finished his last patient - Dr. Noe usually works half-days on Saturdays - and could take me right away. I drove the ten blocks to his building and took the stairs to his 2nd floor office. Dr. Noe has a small practice consisting of himself, a dental assistant, and a receptionist, and his reception area is sized accordingly. I walked in, rang a bell on the reception counter, and looked around for any signs of life. The office is decorated in earth tones - browns, beiges, and a bit of burnt umber thrown in for fun. The furniture is old - vintage 1950s, I'd guess - and hadn't been updated in the 20 years during which I'd been an off-and-on patient. I chose the least uncomfortable chair and sat down to wait.

Marcia, the receptionist, didn't work Saturdays. After a few minutes, Dr. Noe came out of his private office, ushered me into his Chamber of Horrors - he referred to it as his examining room - laid me out on the reclining dental chair, and put a bib on me. He instructed me to "open wide," then shoved a fist-full of probes and mirrors into my mouth before asking, "What seems to be the problem, Damien?"

"Mmmph," I replied.

"Can you be any more specific?"

"Mmph, shrummph," I explained.

He poked and prodded until lightning bolts shot from my mouth to my brain.

"Mmmmph! MMMMPH!"

"Hurts, does it? Well, it looks like you cracked a tooth that already was filled. We'll need a crown to save the tooth. Probably root canal, too."

"Rommmph cmmmph?"

"Jill will take an X-ray. Then we'll know for sure. Don't move."

I lay there with my mouth wide open as Dr. Noe's assistant positioned a piece of X-ray cardboard between my teeth and told me to bite down. Several Roentgens and 20 minutes later, a smiling Dr. Noe reported that I was lucky. "No sign of infection," he said. "We can skip the root canal." He stuck a needle in my gum, took an impression of the cracked tooth, cleaned up the damaged area, and installed a temporary stainless steel crown. He cautioned me not to chew anything harder than a slice of Wonder Bread on that side of my mouth for at least twenty-four hours, and promised that Marcia would call me as soon as my new crown was ready.

It was 3:30 when I left Dr. Noe's office and I was meeting Burt at 6:00. The damned doughnut had put a serious hole in my afternoon - not to mention my bank account. I decided to head over to Happy's a little early. I needed a drink.

I was on my third beer and my second dose of aspirin when Burt walked in. I waved him over and then waggled a finger at the bartender for a couple of fresh drafts. Burt slid into the booth with his back to the entrance. He was wearing a jacket and tie - noticeably overdressed for the place - and looked distinctly uncomfortable. His shoulders hunched as though he was trying to retract his head into an invisible shell.

I thanked him for coming and we made small talk until the waitress who delivered our beers retreated to the bar. He made a point of checking his watch. "Let's make this fast, Dick," he said, a hint of urgency in his voice. "I don't have a lot of time. I'm meeting my wife for dinner." He reached into the breast pocket of his jacket and drew out some folded papers. "Everything you asked for is here." His hand shook slightly as he handed the papers to me.

He started to slide out of the booth. I forestalled him by gripping his left wrist with my right hand. "Wait, Burt."

"It's my job if this gets out, Dick."

"Just a question or two, Burt." He shrugged and sat back down.

"When is Benny due for his next parole check-in?" I asked.

"He was due on Wednesday. He's late." Burt stood again. "And so am I."

He reached for his wallet. I waved him off. "Beer's on me," I said. "Thanks for the dope."

"This cancels all debts, Dick," he replied as he turned to leave. "Don't ask me for anything else."

I watched Burt weave his way rapidly between the tables and out to the street, unfolded the papers, and read them as I sipped my beer. Bruno had been in and out of trouble from the time he was fifteen. Penny-ante stuff: some shop-lifting, a bit of fencing. Nothing violent. Benny was no angel, either, but was better at avoiding detection. His 'sheet' showed a few arrests for moving stolen property, but only one conviction. Until this week, he had been careful to meet his parole conditions, always turning up for his scheduled meetings with Burt. No complaints. Not even a parking ticket.

Both men listed the same person as next-of-kin. Sophia Caravaggio was Bruno's mother and Benny's sister. The files showed her address as 6 Laurel Lane, Everettville, New Jersey, but no phone number. I stuffed the papers into my pocket, tossed some cash on the table, and walked back to my car. According to the trusty AAA map that I extracted from my glove compartment, Everettville was 50 miles northwest of Atlantic City. Just the right distance for a Sunday drive.

Fifteen

I opened my eyes to a vision of thousands of spots dancing in front of my face, and felt my heart skip a beat. How many beers had slid down my throat at Happy's? And how many more after I returned home? I shook myself awake and realized that the dots were particles of dust floating in the morning sun. The bright sunshine streaming through my bedroom window highlighted an abstract pattern of streaks and swirls on the glass that would not have been out of place in a Jackson Pollock painting. The display on my clock radio read 09:00AM. I eased out of bed and staggered into a shower, allowing the randomly varying hot and cold spray to wash the last cobwebs from my brain. I dried off, shaved, and inserted myself into a pair of chinos and a polo shirt. It promised to be another hot day, so I shoved my bare feet into a pair of canvas loafers. Eager to hit the road, I decided that breakfast could wait.

I trotted down the back stairs to the parking lot, slid behind the wheel of the Celica, and rechecked the map. I'd be taking US-30 along the neck of land that separates Absecon Bay from Lakes Bay and connects Atlantic City to the New Jersey mainland. After what looked to be about 30 miles on US-30, I should pick up US-206, which promised to deliver me to Everettville.

There is a cluster of cheap motels, gas stations and fast food outlets where US-30 crosses the Garden State Parkway. I stopped at one of the gas stations to fill up. The doughnut shop next door supplied breakfast - a couple of jelly doughnuts and a large black coffee. I inhaled the doughnuts and washed them down with the coffee before getting back on the road.

About 40 minutes later, I turned off US-206 onto Main Street and drove north through the center of town. Everettville was a prosperous looking village. The houses were mostly clapboard, freshly painted in white with contrasting trim - typically brown or green - and surrounded by close-cropped lawns, and beds of shrubs and flowers. Closer into the center of the village, an occasional brick building relieved the monotony of the architecture. The lamp posts were in full bloom; red, white and blue bunting from which sprouted matching flags on short sticks. Clearly, Independence Day in Everettville lasted the full month of July.

I drove slowly up Main, checking the names of the handful of cross streets. No sign of Laurel Lane. I looked for a place to ask directions. The village had the requisite collection of public facilities: Town Hall at the south end (closed on Sunday), the Everett Memorial Public Library in the center of town (closed on Sunday), Everett's Supermarket (open from 12:00 - 5:00 pm on Sunday), and two churches - the Methodists near the south end of the village and the Baptists guarding the approach from the north. The streets were deserted and the church parking lots only half full. The inhabitants of Everettville were either in church or sleeping off Saturday night.

I followed Main Street past the Baptist church. It led me out of the village and past several farm houses before rejoining US-206. I doubled back and, just north of the village, pulled into the parking lot of Everett's Oil and Propane. I parked next to the only other car in the lot, gave the Celica a gentle double tap on its posterior with my knuckles, and walked over to the office. The door was unlocked, and I walked through into a time warp.

The reception area was furnished in spartan 1950s business modern - a couple of chairs with bare oak seats and straight backs, set on either side of a small square table. The floor covering was vintage linoleum, faded to a washed out gray except for the cracked and darkened area that traced a well-traveled path leading from the door to the 4-foot high reception counter. Facing me from behind the counter was a tall, fleshy, forty-ish man whose name tag identified him as Bob.

"Can I help you?" he asked.

"I hope so. I'm looking for Laurel Lane. Could you give me directions?"

"Well, you're not far," he assured me, as he came out from behind his counter. "Just go past the Baptist Church and take the next right turn. Continue to Sycamore, make a left, then another left onto Oak, a right on Maple, another right on Sumac, and then a left on Laurel. You can't miss it." I nodded, working to keep track of the forest of tree names, muttering Sycamore, Oak, Maple, Sumac, Laurel while I tried to look as though I understood his directions. He noticed my confusion, took pity on me, and drew a rough map on a scrap piece of paper.

"Not too many people are interested in Laurel," Bob commented. "It's a bit out of the way." I shrugged by way of reply. "You're the second person asking for directions," he went on. "Is Sophia having a house party?"

"Sophia?" I asked.

"Yeah. Sophia Caravaggio. The other fellow asked for directions to her place, so I told him how to find her." I was perturbed by this news, and my face must have shown it. "Hope I didn't put my foot in something soft and stinky," he said, wrinkling his forehead. He looked me over slowly, from head to foot. "You from the coast?"

"Yes."

He nodded in satisfaction. "Thought so from your clothes. Most people around here don't go without socks - or wear canvas loafers for that matter."

"Who was asking about Sophia?" I probed.

"Don't know." He shrugged. "The guy wasn't from around here, and he didn't look like a relative either, if you know what I mean."

95

"What did he look like, then?"

"He was a black guy. Taller than me." He raised his arm, palm down, to indicate the height. "Maybe six-four. Hefty. Not fat, though. Muscular, like."

I thanked him, shook hands, and turned to go, the scrap of map firmly clutched in my left fist, silently repeating "Sycamore, Oak, Maple, Sumac, Laurel, Sycamore, Oak, Maple, Sumac, Laurel, Sycamore, Oak....." as I returned to my car.

I followed Bob's map and my nose, and found Laurel Lane after only two wrong turns. It proved to be a dirt road that ran parallel to the south shore of a small lake. Number six was at the end of the road on the south side - the dry side - of the road.

The house was easily the smallest one on Laurel; a little A-frame, probably with a bedroom loft that overlooked the living room. It radiated the air of benign neglect that often attaches to properties occupied by single women of limited means. The forest surrounding the house had been cut back at some point to provide a clear space of about 100 feet around the building. The clearing hadn't been mowed recently; the grass and weeds were thigh high. There was no garage. A 1960s-era VW Beetle was parked in the driveway.

I pulled in behind the VW, parked, and walked up the two steps to the front porch. The screen door was torn and warped. The knotty pine front door had once been stained mahogany. Remnants of the original staining were visible in the pine knots; the rest of the wood had faded almost to its natural pale yellow-white color. I rang the bell and was rewarded by the faint sound of a female voice calling "Just a minute." I looked at my watch. Twelve-fifteen. I was probably interrupting her lunch.

I heard footsteps, then a click, followed by a creak as the door opened a couple of inches. It was on one of those useless security chains that screw into the door and its jamb. The kind of chain designed to make a solitary woman feel safer in her home. The kind of chain that can be dislodged in an instant by a hard shove. The pair of eyes that peered through the crack in the door reminded me of diamonds - the hardest substance on earth, but easily fractured if someone knows how to apply pressure correctly.

"What do you want?"

"Are you Sophia Caravaggio?"

"Who wants to know?" The bravado of her words was belied by the note of fear and suspicion in her voice.

"My name is Damien Dickens," I began.

"Go away!" She slammed the door in my face. I could hear her footsteps echoing across bare floor as she retreated to the back of the house. I decided to see whether I'd have any better luck out of sight of the road. A small screened porch ran the length of the back wall. I walked up the steps and onto the porch. When I knocked on the back door, Sophia didn't even bother to open it. She spoke to me instead through a minuscule opening in the kitchen window. "Why are you still here?" Her voice trembled with a mixture of fear and anger. "Please. Go away and leave us alone."

I couldn't help staring at her. Her face was a female twin for Benny's. Same eyes, same nose, same chin. But Sophia's mouth was prim, her lips pursed tensely. And her hair was salt-and-pepper, not Benny's washed out mousy gray. Her skin, too, was different - bespeaking an outdoor life - tanned, weathered, and wrinkled, unlike Benny's soft skin and lingering prison pallor. She stared defiantly back at me, her head trembling slightly, as I took in her appearance.

"Sophia," I began. I kept my voice gentle; I needed to gain her trust. "You must listen to me. Benny is in danger."

She thought about that for a couple of minutes, then walked over to the back door, unlocked it, and waved me inside. She closed and locked the door, leaned against it and stared at me, her arms folded over her chest. "Well?" she asked.

"Sophia, can we sit? There's a lot to talk about."

She walked over to the kitchen table, pulled out a chair and sat down in front of a half-empty mug of tea, motioning me to take the chair opposite. "Well?" she repeated. "We're sitting now. What do you want?"

"Sophia, I'm trying to find Benny. Someone is after him. He's in danger."

"What's it to you?" Her eyes were scornful and accusing. "You're his nemesis. His bad angel. It was your testimony that sent him to prison. Why do you care what happens to him now?"

"Bruno asked me to help him."

"Bruno?" Her brows furrowed with concern at my mention of her son's name. "Why would Bruno ask for your help?"

"Sophia, there's more." I reached across the table and took her hand. "Bruno was shot."

She jerked her hand back. "By you?"

"No. By the same person who is after Benny." I hesitated, unsure how much to say, then plowed straight on. She looked like a woman who was used to coping with unpleasant news. "Sophia, Bruno is in bad shape. I don't want the same thing to happen to Benny."

Sophia stood abruptly. "Where's Bruno? Where's my son?"

"In Atlantic City."

"Take me to him."

"Of course. But, Benny…"

"Benny's here."

"Here?"

"There's an old shed 'way back in the woods. He's hiding there. Every couple of days, I bring him food and water."

"Sophia, I need to talk to him."

"He doesn't want to see you, Dickens. He doesn't trust you. He doesn't trust anybody. Only me." She grabbed her handbag and started for the door. "Benny's safe enough there. He's well hidden. Now, take me to Bruno."

I saw that it was useless to argue further. I followed Sophia through the house and out the front door, helped her into the passenger seat of the Celica, and retraced the route to Atlantic City. Perhaps Bruno could convince her to trust me. If she was allowed to see him. If he was conscious. If he was still alive.

Sixteen

It took no more than five minutes for me to fill Sophia in on what I knew about Bruno's recent adventures. The rest of the drive to Atlantic City passed in silence. Neither of us was in the mood for small talk. Sophia was worried about Bruno; I was thinking about Benny. I stopped at a gas station near the Garden State Parkway, fished a quarter out of my pocket and used a pay phone to call Gus. He promised to meet us at the hospital and square it for Sophia to see Bruno immediately. I told him I planned to return to Everettville as soon as I delivered Sophia to the hospital; I'd try to convince Benny to come back to the city with me.

Gus was as good as his word. By the time Sophia and I arrived at the Atlantic City Medical Center, he had already spoken to the head of the ICU and smoothed the way for Sophia to stay with Bruno, whose condition remained 'critical but stable.' He also arranged for a police guard on the ICU in case someone decided to make another attempt at silencing Bruno. I left Sophia staring at her son through a plate glass window, and headed back to Everettville. Traffic was light, and I ignored the posted speed limits. It was just after 5pm when I turned into Sophia's driveway for the second time. There were still three hours until sunset - plenty of time to explore the woods behind Sophia's house.

I walked the perimeter of the clearing until I found a path that entered the woods. I had followed it for a few hundred yards, watching for any sign of life or lodging, when my eye was caught by a large boot print in a patch of drying mud. It wasn't Benny's - he was too small to have such large feet. I compared it to the size of my own shoe. I wear a 10½; this print had to be at least a size 12. I skirted the area, taking care not to disturb the impression of the boot in the hardening mud. My pace quickened; a sense of danger prickled the hairs on the back of my neck. The main path curved to the left, while a narrower footpath branched off to the right. I followed the right fork deeper into the woods, and found myself facing the blank rear wall of a small cabin.

The building - little more than a shack - was constructed out of rough, unpainted planks. The shallow-pitched shake roof was punctuated by a narrow stovepipe near one end. A pile of firewood was stacked neatly against the side of the cabin. My nose caught the characteristic perfume of *eau de outhouse* - an aroma comprising equal parts of disinfectant and decomposing body waste. I glanced to my right. Sure enough, I could see the source of the odor about 100 feet away. I walked around to the front of the cabin.

The front door was open and askew - hanging by a single hinge. I stopped short, automatically reaching for my gun, before I remembered that I wasn't carrying one. I returned to the woodpile and selected a log that would serve as a weapon of sorts. Gripping it tightly in my right hand, I eased into the cabin and looked around. No sign of life, except for the swarm of flies that were buzzing about a half-eaten bowl of cereal on the kitchen table. The chair was toppled over onto its side, a large rust-brown stain on the floor nearby.

I backed away, trying not to disturb anything. As I left the cabin, I noticed a pair of shallow parallel lines etched in the dirt, pointing toward the forest. On a hunch, I followed their track, walking a couple of feet to the side to avoid stepping on them. The lines disappeared once they entered the woods, to be replaced by a trail of torn twigs and mashed mulch. That trail led to another clearing, at the far end of which was a large house. One of Sophia's well-heeled neighbors, no doubt. Once out of the woods, the trail was harder to follow, but I could see the remnants of parallel lines gouged into the tall grass. I followed the lines to the top of a small mound and found myself standing on top of a buried septic tank. I had reached the end of the trail.

I stood for a few minutes, staring at the lid of the tank. I knew what I had to do. I knelt down and used the grip holes to turn the manhole cover counterclockwise. It gave easily. I removed the cover, extracted a penlight flashlight from my pocket, and shone it into the tank. I reeled back, stunned by the stench and by the sight of a pair of unblinking eyes that stared back at me from a familiar face. I had found Benny.

I scrambled to my feet, ran to the house, and pummeled on the door until someone opened it so abruptly that I narrowly missed punching him in the face. "Call 9-1-1!" I gasped. "Murder. Dead body. Septic tank."

I realized how ludicrous I must have sounded when I saw his incredulous look an instant before he slammed the door in my face. I took a moment to compose myself, extracted a business card from my wallet, and knocked on the door again. It opened slightly, and I shoved my card through the crack. "Look," I said. "I'm a private detective. My name is Damien Dickens. This is not a prank. There's a dead man in your septic tank. Please call 9-1-1."

He looked at my card and stepped outside, closing the door carefully behind him. He was a medium sort of guy: medium height, medium weight, medium brown hair cut to a medium length that hovered about a quarter inch above the collar of his beige polo shirt. "My name is Dewsen," he said. "I'm the County Sheriff. Why don't you show me this dead man that you say you found."

I walked him over to the septic tank. We peered inside as I shone my light on Benny's face. He gasped and stepped back. "You stay here and make sure nothing disturbs the body. I'll call this in." I crouched down a short distance from the open tank, watching his receding back and wishing that I was someplace else. Any place else.

He returned in just a few minutes. "The crime scene team will be here shortly." He pulled out a notebook and ballpoint pen. "Why don't you tell me what you know while we're waiting? First, do you know who this guy is?"

"I believe so. I'll know for sure when I can get a better look at his face. But I think it's Benny Caravaggio."

He pursed his eyebrows at the sound of the name. "Related to Sophia?" he asked.

I nodded. "Her brother. His name is Benedetto, but he goes by Benny."

"What's the story?"

I gave him the short version, focussing on the part that began with Bruno's shooting. By the time I was done, the team had arrived and was preparing to winch Benny out of the tank. I waited until they finished the grisly task, then confirmed Benny's identity for the Sheriff.

"Now show me how you found him."

I led the Sheriff and a couple of his deputies back along the trail to the cabin and then showed them the footprint I had found on the path between the cabin and Sophia's house.

"And you say that there was a tall black guy also looking for him?" Dewsen asked.

"I think so. At least, he was looking for Sophia," I clarified. "Bob at the propane company was the one who told me about him."

Dewsen made a note. "We'll talk to Bob."

"Look, Sheriff. Can I leave now?"

"Why?"

"It's getting late, and I have an appointment tomorrow morning in Atlantic City. At the D.A.'s office. And I'd like to see Sophia before then to break the news to her about Benny."

"Better you than me." Dewsen shrugged. "Guess we don't need you here anymore tonight. Your phone number on this card?" I nodded, took the card back from him and added my home number and Gus's office number. "One of these will find me. The last number is my attorney's office."

"OK, you can go."

I didn't wait to be told twice. I walked briskly back to my car and drove away from Laurel Lane before Dewsen could change his mind. How do I tell Sophia, I thought, as I navigated the roads, the spears of light from my headlights piercing the dark. How do I break the news? It was after midnight by the time I hit the Garden State Parkway intersection; far too late to go to the hospital. With a guilty sense of reprieve, I pointed the car for home.

I managed a few hours of disjointed sleep, Benny's unblinking eyes accusing me in my dreams. I crawled out of bed at six, and stood under the shower for ten minutes, trying to wash the fog of fatigue from my brain. Even here, I could see Benny's eyes in the pattern made by the small, round, gray ceramic tiles on the bathroom floor. There was no point in further delay. I dressed, swallowed a glass of orange juice, and headed over to the hospital. My feet dragged as I approached the ICU. I walked up to the nurses' station and asked for Sophia.

"She's with her son." The nurse, whose name tag proclaimed her to be Andrea, smiled invitingly as she pointed toward Bruno's cubicle. "You can go in, if you like."

I walked down the hall, my footsteps echoing a tapping rhythm on the linoleum tile floor that seemed to proclaim, "Benny's dead. Benny's dead." There was a cop on guard outside the room. I showed him my driver's license. He checked his list of names, and opened the door to the room. Sophia was sitting beside Bruno's bed; Gus's secretary, Barbara, was standing nearby, stirring the contents of two styrofoam cups. And Bruno? Bruno was awake - eyes open and alert. He was still hooked up to enough monitors to manage a moon shot, but at least he was clearly alive.

Bruno was the first to spot me, his welcoming smile fading as he sensed the news I was bringing. "It's Benny, isn't it?" I nodded in reply, swallowing hard.

"I'm sorry, Sophia; sorry Bruno." I turned to each of them in turn. "I was too late."

Sophia emitted a sound that was somewhere between a moan and a growl. Her body shook with violent sobs. Barbara walked over and put an arm around Sophia's shoulder while Bruno reached for her hand, pleading, "Don't cry, Mom."

Sophia's sobs subsided into a few residual hiccoughs as she struggled to regain control. She lifted her head and turned her tear-stained face toward me. "How did it happen?" I gave her an abbreviated version, then asked her when she had last seen Benny. "I brought him food and water Saturday evening - enough to last for a few days," she said. "It's my fault he's dead. I insisted that you bring me here first. You might have been able to save him."

"Sophia, we don't know yet when he died. From the look of the cabin, I think he was in the middle of breakfast. There was a half-eaten bowl of cereal on the table. I didn't even get to your place until after noon."

"It's still my fault," she insisted, her tears starting to trickle once more. "His killer probably followed me to the cabin on Saturday. I should have been more careful."

I looked up at Bruno, wondering what else I could do or say. He motioned me to go. I mumbled something about looking in on them later and made my escape. There was nothing more I could do for Sophia. Not then.

106

Seventeen

I went for a walk and returned to the hospital after about a half hour. Barbara was leaving as I mounted the steps to the main entrance. She looked worried. "Better get upstairs, Dick," she said. "I didn't want to go, but Sophia asked me to leave her alone for a while. I'll check in at the office and come back later if Mr. C. doesn't need me for anything."

I went upstairs and found Sophia sitting beside Bruno's empty bed, her head buried in her hands. "What's wrong?" I placed my hand on her shoulder. "Where's Bruno?"

Startled, she raised her tear-stained face to look at me. "They took him for additional x-rays," she explained. "He was getting jabs of pain whenever he tried to move. The doctor is concerned that he might still have a bullet fragment inside him." She stood and started to pace. "He's all I have left," she said, wringing her hands as she walked back and forth across the eight-by-eight room. "He's all I have." She stopped abruptly, her face ash white. She was swaying from left to right. As her knees started to buckle, I put my arm around her waist to steady her and guided her over to a chair.

"Have you had anything to eat this morning?" I asked.

She shook her head in response. "I'm not hungry."

"You need to eat," I urged. "Starving yourself won't help Bruno."

She rested her elbows on her thighs and cradled her head in her hands for a few minutes, then sighed. "I guess you're right, Dickens."

"The name's Damien. Let me treat you to what passes for a gourmet breakfast in the hospital cafeteria." She hesitated, then nodded. I put my hand under her elbow and urged her to her feet. "We'll let them know at the nurses' station where they can find us."

After pausing briefly to speak to the nurse at the counter, I led Sophia to the bank of elevators, and we headed to the cafeteria. For some reason, most hospital cafeterias are located on the basement level just down the hall from the morgue. Atlantic City Medical Center was no exception to this rule. Fortunately, the institutional smell of the cafeteria food masked the faint whiff of cadaverine laced with formaldehyde that infiltrated from the hallway. I filled my tray with eggs, hash browns, toast, and coffee; Sophia decided on a cup of tea and some plain toast. We found a quiet table in a corner far from the door and sat down. I started on my scrambled eggs, while Sophia took a minuscule sip of her tea. I put down my fork, and looked directly at her. "Do you want to talk?" I asked.

"About what?"

"About Bruno," I suggested. "Is there anyone we should notify about his condition? His father, perhaps?"

She snorted. "He's the last person I'd tell."

"Would it help to talk about it?"

Sophia shrugged. I sat quietly and waited for her to say something. Anything. Finally, she sighed. "We met at Princeton," she began. "I was in my senior year - majoring in graphic arts, with a minor in marketing - and he was in his last year of law school." She smiled slightly, and closed her eyes, remembering how it was.

"The first time I saw him, he was walking across the quad, heading for the library." Her voice was soft, dreamy, as the memory came flooding back. I could see and hear echoes of a young Sophia, smitten by a handsome stranger. "He was tall, dark, and gorgeous. And he had an air of self-confidence, almost of arrogance, about him. I was sitting on one of the benches, talking to my girlfriend. I remember asking her who he was. 'Don't even think it,' she told me. 'He's a heart-breaker. They call him Mr. Love-Em-and-Leave-Em.' " Sophia stopped to nibble at her toast and take another sip of tea, then continued. "The next time I saw him was in the cafeteria. I was working behind the counter - I had a scholarship to cover the tuition, but I worked a couple of part-time jobs to pay for my room and board. He walked up to my station just as I was putting a fresh tray of lasagna in the display case. 'Are you new here?' he asked me. I told him that I had just started that job the week before. We chatted briefly, and then he moved on. But he was waiting for me when my shift ended, and asked me to have a cup of coffee with him.

"We started dating regularly," she went on. "Barney was from a well-to-do family. He took me to plays, concerts, fine restaurants. Places I'd never have experienced otherwise. He had his own apartment off campus. One evening, after the theatre, he invited me up for a drink. I spent the night." Sophia paused, looking down into her cup, then raised her head and held my gaze. "It was my first time ever. I was in love. For the next couple of months, we continued dating, although we didn't go out as much - just spent time in his apartment." She smiled wryly. "You see, he didn't need to woo me any more - he had achieved his goal." She looked back down at her hands, her words coming faster now, as though she was trying to outrace her memories. "After a while, we didn't see each other as often. I was snowed under with school work and so was he. Then he stopped calling altogether. I thought I had done something to make him angry, so I sent him a note. He never answered. He lived alone; there was no one to take phone messages if he was out. And he always seemed to be out. I spotted him a couple of times on campus, but he would turn away when he saw me approaching him. Then I saw him with another student; they were laughing and embracing under the big oak tree on the quad. I knew then. Off with the old and on with the new. Mr. Love-Em-and-Leave-Em had struck again." She paused again, and I waited quietly for her to continue. "I managed to put him out of my mind," she went on, "and buckled down to complete my last semester. Then, a few weeks before graduation, I discovered that I was pregnant.

"I sent him another letter, telling him that I had to see him. Had to discuss something important with him. That got his attention - he must have guessed from the tone of the letter. He called and we arranged to meet for coffee. When I told him I was pregnant, he asked me who the father was. I told him it was his baby. 'Are you sure?' he asked me. I told him that I was 100% sure - he was the only man I had ever been with. He stood up without another word, and walked away. Didn't even have the courtesy to pay for the coffee." Sophia was crying quietly now, reliving the hurt. I reached into my pocket for a tissue and held it out to her. She took it, and twisted it around in her hands as she went on with her story. "A week later," she said, "I received a letter from an attorney - Barney's attorney. It said that 'their client' was acknowledging the information I had imparted, but was not admitting to responsibility for my unfortunate condition. That's what they called my pregnancy - an unfortunate condition." Sophia paused to deliver a bitter smile and take another sip of tea before continuing. "Nevertheless, the letter said, 'their client' was concerned for my welfare and had instructed the law firm to set up a small trust fund, should the baby - the 'issue', they called it in their letter - survive, and should I decide to raise it myself. The interest from the fund would be paid to me monthly; the principal would be paid in a lump sum to the 'issue' when it - they actually referred to my baby as an 'it' - reached its 25th birthday. I was not to reveal the source of the funds to anyone. The letter instructed me to countersign if I accepted the conditions and return the countersigned original to them. They even provided a stamped, self-addressed envelope for my convenience. I did what they asked. I signed the letter and sent it back." Sophia looked up, dried tears staining her cheeks. "That was twenty-four years ago. The

110

first check arrived the following week. They still turn up in my mail box the first of every month. I've deposited all of the checks into a special account in Bruno's name. I used some of the money to pay for medical expenses, first for the pregnancy, then for Bruno. I never used a penny of Barney's hush money for myself." Sophia held her head high now, proud in her independence. "When Bruno turns twenty-five," she proclaimed, "I'll tell him about the trust fund and hand the bank book to him. There's a tidy sum in it now. He'll be able to make something of himself."

We sat silent for a few minutes. Her story told, Sophia lapsed into a gray study, the fatigue and stress of the last 48 hours showing in her face and posture. I stood and suggested that we return to Bruno's room. As the elevator doors opened on the third floor, we saw an orderly wheeling a gurney down the hall. Bruno was propped up and waved us over. "X-rays were clear," he announced, holding out a hand for Sophia to squeeze. I rested my hand briefly on Bruno's shoulder, promised to drop by later, and left them alone together.

Eighteen

Gus and I had a 9:00am date with District Attorney George Nicholby at the Atlantic City Courthouse. I decided to walk over in order to clear my head. Ten minutes later, I was sitting with Gus and Nicholby in a small interview room that was furnished with a rectangular table boasting a faux-wood laminate top, bolted to industrial strength metal legs. The table could seat six people in a pinch, but we weren't planning on a full house.

Gus and the D.A. made sporadic small talk as we waited for the evidence clerk to arrive with the files we had requested. I was too antsy to make a pretense of polite conversation; the room brought back memories of my recent interrogation by Sherlock and Holmes. There was a tap on the door, and we all turned in anticipation. But it was only a go-fer who had fetched coffee at Nicholby's request. I went through the ritual of adding sugar and powdered fake cream, stirred assiduously, sipped politely, and faintly praised the bitter brown slop. It helped pass the time.

Ten minutes later, we heard another tap on the door, followed by a thump as the evidence clerk used his wheeled cart to push his way into the room. The clerk pointed with a flourish toward the two official-looking file boxes that rode the top shelf of the cart, as he held out a clipboard in Nicholby's direction. The D.A. signed the receipt that was clipped to the board and handed it back to the clerk, who admonished us not to remove any of the contents of the boxes from the room, and to call him when we were done. We could hear the latch click into place as the door swung shut on its hinges.

Nicholby watched with a bemused smile as Gus and I removed file after file from the first box. We hit pay dirt in the penultimate file folder, where we found the creased original of the typed ransom note that I was alleged to have sent to Celine the night of her murder. The envelope in which it was delivered was nowhere to be found. The second box contained items that the cops had collected when they searched my office. In it were all of my office files that made even a passing reference to the Sutherland family or to Sutherland Smokes. A separate folder in the same box held the loose papers taken from the desk tops, waste baskets, and chair seats. In it, I found the originals of the two rough drafts of the purported ransom note. I cleared a space on the table top and laid out all three versions of the note side by side. Gus opened his briefcase, extracted the note that I had found under the Boardwalk near where Celine's body was discovered, unfolded it and placed it on the table next to the other three. I took a pocket magnifier out of my jacket and examined all four sheets of paper. I could feel a stirring of excitement in my gut. I handed the lens across the table. "Gus, look at this and tell me what you think."

He scrutinized each sheet of paper in turn, twice, then looked up at me and nodded. "I think you're right, Dick."

The D.A. leaned forward. "Right about what?"

Gus shook his head. "Later." He picked up the note that I had found under the Boardwalk, refolded it carefully and returned it to his briefcase. "I think we're done for now."

As Nicholby buzzed for the evidence clerk to have the boxes removed, Gus turned to me. "Why don't you drop by the office later today, Dick," he suggested. "There's something I need to discuss with George, here."

That suited me fine. The room was getting claustrophobic. Besides, I had work to do. Witnesses to interview. A killer to track down. I left the courthouse and walked back to the hospital, where I had left my car. I detoured upstairs to check on Bruno, hoping he'd be up for a chat, but the nurse at the desk told me - rather sternly,

I thought - that he was sleeping and should not be disturbed. I asked for Sophia, but she was asleep on a couch in Bruno's room. She'd had a rough couple of days and needed the rest.

I retrieved my car from the Visitor's parking lot and drove the few blocks over to Boardwalk Hall, the home of the two social highlights of every Atlantic City summer - the Christmas in July Charity Ball and the September Miss America Pageant. I introduced myself to the receptionist and asked to see the manager. After I'd spent several minutes cooling my heels in front of a giant poster of Susan Perkins, the reigning Miss America, being crowned by Phyllis George and serenaded by Bert Parks, a roly-poly figure walked up to me. If Tweedledum and Tweedledee had been triplets, this fellow would have passed for the third brother. He was no more than 5'6" tall even in his Elevators shoes. His face was round, his cheeks were pink, and his torso was almost as broad as it was long. He was nattily dressed in a royal blue suit with a navy pinstripe and a white silk shirt with French cuffs that were secured by gold cufflinks. His paisley foulard was pouf'd out to fill the V-shaped void defined by the open neck of his shirt. An aura of sweet cologne formed an invisible cloud around him as he held out his manicured hand to me and introduced himself as Stephane Major, pronouncing his given name with the accent on the second syllable.

I handed him my card and explained that I was investigating the Celine Sutherland murder. "How can I help?" he asked, looking up at me with his head cocked slightly to one side.

"I need to talk to members of your staff who were in attendance the night of the Christmas in July ball. I'm hoping that someone might have seen or spoken with the messenger who delivered an envelope addressed to Miss Sutherland during the ball."

"Well," he simpered as he puffed out his chest. "That would be me. I'm always on duty for that event. It would never do to have an underling represent the management for the social event of the year, *n'est ce pas?*"

I don't know French, but I assumed that *n'est ce pas* was a verbal tic, in the same category as 'like' and 'you know.' "Of course." I nodded in reply. "Did you happen to see the messenger?"

"My good man, I was at the entrance when he arrived. I circulated through the entire facility every fifteen minutes to keep my eye on the *arrangements*. One cannot take anything for granted, can one?"

He gave a French pronunciation to arrangements, rolling the double 'r', softening the 'g' and stretching the word into four syllables. This guy was starting to get under my skin. "No, I guess one cannot." I hoped he would detect the irony in my voice, and I wished in passing that I could have watched Sherlock interrogate this guy. "What did he look like?" I asked.

"Who?"

"The messenger. What did he look like?"

"Well." He gestured with one hand, palm up and wrist bent back at an unnatural angle. "That's difficult to say. It was rather dark near the door. I do recall that he was wearing a uniform and cap."

"What kind of uniform?"

"Oh, ill-cut and cheap-looking, don't you know. The jacket was a rather nondescript brown; the sleeves were too short and the trousers needed pressing."

I took a deep breath and tried again. "So it was light enough to see the color of his uniform. What about his face? Would you recognize him?"

"My good man. Why ever would I remember his face? He was just a messenger, n'est ce *pas?*" I winced as Major touched me lightly on my forearm for emphasis. Patience, I told myself. Patience. You need his cooperation.

"What about his voice? Did he say anything or just gesture?"

Major giggled. "My, you're quite droll, aren't you. Of course he said something. He had a very twangy voice - like a banjo tuned too tightly."

I gritted my teeth and gave Mr. Major another verbal nudge. "What did he say?"

"Well!" An indignant flounce entered Major's voice. "When I noticed him at the door, I went over and asked if I could be of assistance. He was quite abrupt. He just asked right out for Mr. Gordon Sethwick. No finesse."

"What happened next?"

"Mr. Sethwick was standing nearby, as it happened. I called him over and the messenger handed him the envelope and left."

"What did Mr. Sethwick do?"

"Well." Major paused again. "He looked at the envelope and walked back towards the party. The silent auction was about to begin. I happened to be walking in the same direction." He nodded with a slight smile. "My fifteen-minute rounds, *n'est ce pas?*"

"And?"

"Mr. Sethwick walked over to Miss Celine and gave her the envelope."

"Did you happen to see what Miss Celine did?"

"Yes. She opened the envelope and extracted a sheet of paper from it."

"What did she do then?"

"Well." Major indulged himself in a small shrug, releasing a cloud of cologne in my direction. "She read the note and went very pale - antique white, I'd say. Then she put the note into her evening bag, said something to Mr. Sethwick, and fairly flew out of the ballroom like Cinderella at midnight."

"What time was this?"

"The silent auction was scheduled to begin at 10:30pm, so it would have been shortly before that time, *n'est ce pas?*"

"What kind of evening bag was she carrying?" I asked.

"Oh, it was green - studded with a magnificent pattern of emeralds. A bit flashy for my taste, but beautiful, nonetheless."

"What about the envelope? What happened to it?"

"I think Miss Celine dropped it on the floor while she was reading the note. I saw Mr. Sethwick stoop down to pick something up as she ran off."

"Just one more question, Mr. Major."

"Yes?" He leaned forward eagerly.

"What did Mr. Sethwick do after Miss Celine ran out?"

"Oh." He deflated - clearly disappointed. Perhaps he was hoping I would ask him to join me for coffee. He thought for a moment, then his expression brightened back into its professional pose. "Oh yes. Mr. Sethwick started to follow Miss Celine, but Miss Sylvia stopped him. She took him by the arm and they walked together to the auctioneer to start the silent auction."

I thanked him for his help. He beamed as though he had just aced his college entrance exams and laid his hand on my forearm. "My pleasure, I'm sure," he purred. I extracted myself from his gentle but insistent grasp and returned to my car. I knew where I was going next.

Nineteen

I exited the Boardwalk Hall parking lot, hung a right onto Pacific Avenue and a left onto S. Arkansas. The traffic was light, and I found myself on the Atlantic City Expressway before I could say 'Gordon Sethwick'. I took Exit 5 off the expressway, headed north on New Road, and turned left onto W. Delilah. My destination was a two-story industrial building at the corner of Canale and Parkway Drive. I was fiddling with the radio, trying to find a newscast, when I stumbled on WMID's 'Sounds of the 60s' and the opening bars of Tom Jones' big hit of 1968. I snapped the radio off as Tom began asking, "Why, why, why, Delilah?" and almost missed Canale Drive.

The Sutherland Industrial Park, which is tucked into a corner formed where the Atlantic City Expressway crosses over the Garden State Parkway, is the home of Sutherland Smokes, Inc. The Sutherland complex of manufacturing, warehousing, and distribution buildings accounts for about one quarter of the industrial park. Old Man Sutherland never believed in wasting money on ostentatious exteriors, but current management had different ideas. The headquarters building had been clad in a silvery metal veneer; immense emerald green letters mounted above the top row of windows spelled out 'Sutherland Smokes, Inc.' A large sign that had been recently planted in the front lawn to the right of the main entrance displayed the company's logo - a green pearl set on a platinum-colored oyster half-shell. Below the logo was a statement reminding passers-by that this was the corporate home of Sutherland Smokes, Inc. A discrete notice on the wall to the left of the entrance instructed visitors to register with the receptionist. There was no one at the front desk, so I took that as an invitation to take the stairs directly up to the second floor.

The suite of executive offices was at the far end of a long hallway that had all the panache of a New York

119

subway platform. The hall was lit with fluorescent tubes that flickered in random patterns guaranteed to provoke headaches and eyestrain. The walls were painted an institutional gray, and hung with advertising posters for Sutherland products. The floor was finished in green and white linoleum tiles displaying a swirl motif.

I reached the end of the corridor and confronted a mahogany-stained solid wood door on which were stenciled the words 'Executive Offices' in green lettering. Underneath, in smaller letters, was the admonition 'By Appointment Only.' I opened the door and walked into a different world. The floors of the executive suite were thickly carpeted in a medium pile wool of forest green. The walls were wainscoted, with mahogany paneling below and silver-flecked pastel green wallpaper above. Decorative incandescent wall sconces and semi-flush incandescent ceiling fixtures provided comfortable illumination. All of the desks were mahogany-stained to match the paneling; all of the chairs - even the secretarial chairs - were padded and upholstered in leather. It was lunchtime, and the area seemed deserted.

I walked the perimeter of the room until I reached an open door beside which was affixed a green plaque with silver lettering identifying this to be the 'Office of the Vice President, Finance.' I peered inside. A slender, blond woman was standing at a file cabinet, her back to me. She turned around when I rapped on the door jamb, and gasped. It was Millie. We stared at each other for an eternity. She looked good. She looked very good. She was wearing one of those 'dressed for success' business suits - a tidy pearl gray outfit with a frilly white blouse.

"What are you doing here, Dick? You shouldn't be here." Her voice was tense.

"Nice to see you, too, Millie." I allowed a touch of sarcasm to enter my voice. I hadn't forgiven her for deserting me. "I see you're moving up the corporate ladder rather efficiently."

She shrugged off my barb. "I'm filling in for Mr. Sethwick's permanent secretary. She's on vacation." She paused. "You're looking tired, Dick. Are you taking care of yourself?"

I ignored the olive branch. "Is your boss in?"

"Yes, but..."

"Is he with someone?"

"No, but..."

Before she could voice her objection, I was across the room and opening the door to Sethwick's inner office. He looked up from the papers on his desk as I approached, his face registering surprise and annoyance. And something more. Something that I couldn't put my finger on. Before either of us could speak, Millie rushed into the room. "I'm sorry, Mr. Sethwick." She sounded slightly out of breath. "I tried to stop him, but he bulled right past me."

Sethwick nodded an acknowledgment and waved her off. "It's OK, Millie," he said. "I'll call you if I need you." Then he turned to me. "I've been expecting you," he said. "Let's get this over with." Sethwick motioned me to one of the upholstered leather seats and we stared at each other in silence across his desk. He broke eye contact first, and started toying with a glass paperweight shaped like a box of cigarettes. The green and platinum Sutherland logo was embedded in the top surface of the glass. "I have an appointment in ten minutes," he said, gesturing at the imposing grandfather clock centered on the wall to his right. "What do you want?"

"I have a couple of questions," I replied, "about the night Celine was killed."

I saw a brief spasm flicker across his face at the mention of her name. "And what if I don't want to answer?"

"I can't force you," I admitted with a shrug.

Sethwick sighed. "OK, go ahead."

"Thanks." I took a deep breath and dove in. "About the message that was delivered to Celine the night of the ball."

"What about it?"

"I'm told that the messenger asked for you by name. I'm wondering why. Was your name on the envelope?"

"No. The envelope said 'Celine Sutherland.' "

"So how did you enter into the picture?"

"How the hell should I know?" Sethwick's voice rose a few decibels, and his face reddened. "Look. I told this to the police when I made my statement. Read their damn report, why don't you!"

"I did. But I need to hear it from you first hand." I held up my hands, palms forward. "Look. No need to get your shirt ruffled. I'm just trying to get straight in my mind what happened."

He nodded in acknowledgment and motioned brusquely for me to continue.

"What about the messenger?" I asked. "Can you tell me anything about him?"

"Like what, for instance?"

"Like, what did he look like? For instance."

"I didn't really pay attention. He wore a uniform - brown, I think - but I didn't notice any insignia." He shrugged. "He was just a messenger. I doubt that I'd recognize him. It was too dark to get a good look at his face."

"Did he say anything to you?"

"No. Just handed me the envelope and left."

"Then what did you do with it?"

"I saw that it was addressed to Celine, so I gave it to her."

"How did she react?"

"She opened the envelope, read the note, shoved it into her evening bag, and left."

"Did she seem upset?" This was as frustrating as the interview with the Boardwalk Hall manager.

"She went pale when she read the note. So, yes, I'd say she was upset."

"Where did she go when she left?"

"I don't know. I thought to follow her, but I had to stay to start the silent auction." He glanced at his Rolex, then looked pointedly at the grandfather clock. "Anything else?"

"Just one more thing." I paused and looked him straight in the eyes. "Why did you come to my office asking about Celine the Monday after the ball?"

He dropped his eyes and fidgeted with the paperweight again. "I knew she had consulted you about something. I thought, maybe, you'd have an idea where she was." Sethwick was hiding something. I could tell. His mouth was telling one story, and his body was speaking a different language. But he wasn't going to give me a chance to probe any further. He stood and pointed me to the door. "It's time for you to leave," he said, his voice cold enough to freeze the entire Jersey Shore. "Your ten minutes are up."

I strode out of Sethwick's office, lobbing a curt nod in Millie's general direction as I passed her desk, and crossed the expanse of outer office. As I approached the door that would lead me back into the 2ⁿᵈ floor hallway, a severely-dressed woman walked past me as though I was a piece of office furniture. I turned to watch as Sylvia Sutherland strode unceremoniously into Sethwick's private office. She cut off his automatic greeting with a gesture, and an abrupt, "What was he doing here?" Sethwick shook his head in warning, and motioned her to shut the door. I felt Millie's eyes on me, so I flung a second nod at her and walked out.

Twenty

I drove back to the city, feeling frustrated and disturbed at the outcome of my interview with Sethwick. I don't know what I had hoped for - although a confession would have been nice - but I'd left his office empty-handed. I decided to head back to the hospital before stopping by to see Gus. Perhaps Bruno would be awake and in a mood to answer some questions.

I left the car in the Visitor's parking lot and trod the now familiar route to the ICU. When I asked for Bruno, I was told that he had been moved to a regular floor. I followed the nurse's directions to Bruno's new home away from home. He was lodged in a private room, with a police guard on the door. I gave the officer my name and was waved inside. And there was Bruno, sitting propped up in bed like a pasha surrounded by his courtiers: Sophia at his right hand, her eyes never leaving his face, Barbara on his left, steno pad in hand, Gus and the D.A. standing next to each other at the foot of his bed.

Gus turned his head as I walked in. "Hi Dick," he greeted me. "Good timing. We're just about done here." He turned to Barbara. "Type that up and bring it back here for Bruno to read and sign. Have one of the nurses or doctors witness Bruno's signature. And notarize it, too, just for good measure. When you're done, get copies made for Bruno and me, and deliver the original to Mr. Nicholby personally." He turned to the D.A. "Does that work for you, George?"

"Sounds good to me."

"Good." Gus nodded in satisfaction. "Top priority, Barb. I want this done today."

Barbara was already halfway out the room, her "I'm on it, Mr. C." trailing in her wake.

125

Nicholby held out his hand to me. "Nice to see you again, Dickens. Sorry, but I have to rush off to a meeting. I'm sure Gus will fill you in."

I turned to Gus. "What just happened?" He smiled. "Gotta go, Dick. I'm late for an appointment. Come by the office after you're done here, and I'll bring you up to speed." And he was gone, too.

I looked at Sophia and Bruno. "Isn't anyone going to tell me what's going on?"

Sophia opened her mouth to reply, but Bruno jumped in first. "Mom, why don't you leave me alone with Mr. Dickens for a few minutes?"

"Are you sure, honey?" she asked. "You're not too tired?"

"I'm OK, Mom. Honest. Now go. Get some coffee or something. And close the door, please."

Bruno and I watched as Sophia closed the door carefully behind her. "You're looking better, Bruno," I said by way of opening the conversation.

"Thanks, Pop." He smiled. "You don't mind if I call you Pop, do you?" He pointed to a chair. "Have a seat, d'you mind? It hurts my head to look up for long."

"Sure, Bruno." I pulled up a chair and sat. "You want to tell me what's going on?"

He nodded carefully. "That's why I asked you to stay. What's going on is that I had a long talk with Mom about what happened to Uncle Benny and me, and how you got suckered into this. She said she'd stand by me if I came clean. So I did. I told the full story to Mr. Augustus (I understand why he prefers 'Gus' - I'd hate to be called 'Julius' all the time) and then to Mr. Nicholby for the record. I've come clean and I'm going to stay clean."

I opened my mouth, but he waved me off. "Look. We only have a few minutes until the nurse comes in to check on me. I want to get this off my chest. You deserve to hear it from me. Maybe tomorrow you can come back and we can talk longer."

I nodded. "OK, Bruno."

Here's what happened," he began. "I was approached by one of the bikers I used to hang out with. Big black guy. Name's Cosmo. He said he had a job for me, if I could get Benny and the other pawnbroker in town - you know who I mean - to play along."

"The evening bag scam." I interjected.

"That's right. Only, he didn't tell me who would be bringing the bag to the store, or that someone would break into Benny's shop, trash the place, and steal the bag if you left it there. And beating up on poor Uncle Benny wasn't part of the package either."

"Why did you continue to play along?"

"I was scared he'd hurt Benny even worse. Cosmo's a bad dude - he's a collector for a local loan shark. He threatened to kill us both if we squealed. When you came into the shop looking for the evening bag, Cosmo was in the back room with Benny, holding a knife to his throat. So I kept my trap shut and did what I was told. But Benny was real pissed off. Cosmo had trashed both him and his shop; Benny started making noises about going to the cops after you left. That night, someone tried to break in again. Benny called 9-1-1 and the sirens scared off whoever it was."

"Is that why you sent me the note asking for help?"

"Yeah. I dropped the note through your mail slot Friday morning. Benny lit out that same day. He was too scared to hang around any longer."

Bruno's voice was starting to drag. I could tell he was tiring, so I stood to go. "I'll come by tomorrow and we can talk more," I said. "But answer this for me. Were you also the messenger and the fake cop?"

He nodded.

"And are you the one who slugged me?"

"No, Pop." He shook his head, then winced from a jab of pain. "Not me. That might have been Cosmo, but I don't know for sure." I held out my right hand, and he gripped it in both of his. "I'm sorry, Pop," he said. "Real sorry to have made such a mess of things."

The door to the room opened, revealing Sophia and a nurse. "Don't sweat it, Bruno." I freed my hand. "I'll be back tomorrow," I assured him as I turned to leave, feeling better than at any time in the days since Celine was killed.

Part of me wanted to drop into Happy's and celebrate Bruno's transformation. But I had promised Gus I'd come by. It was nearly five o'clock when I walked into his outer office. Barbara's fingers were flying over her typewriter keys, creating a perfect symphony of clicks, clacks, bells and whirrs, her eyes focussed on her steno pad. She looked up briefly and smiled. "Go right in, Dick. He's expecting you."

I opened the door to the inner sanctum. Gus was sitting at his desk. His jacket was off, his tie - he was sporting Yale's blue and white color scheme today - was loose, and the top two buttons of his pinstripe button-down shirt were undone. He had his shoes off and his argyle-clad feet were propped on his desk blotter. "Hey, Dick." He waved at me. "Grab a chair. Make yourself comfortable. Want a beer?"

"Sure. What's the occasion?"

"You are." He handed me a can of Samuel Adams. "Bruno's got you off the hook, you dumb goof."

"What do you mean by 'off the hook?' "

"Nicholby says that if Bruno's statement checks out, they'll drop the charges against you."

I sat, stunned. The charges and bail restrictions hanging over me had become my new normal.

"What's the matter," Gus asked, a little peeved at my silence. "You have a problem with that?"

I shook my head. "No. Just needed to digest it a little. That's great news, Gus."

Barbara rapped on the door and stuck her head into the room. "I'm done with the statement, Mr. C." she announced. "Want to check it before I leave?"

"No." Gus waved her off. "I trust you. Just make sure Bruno reads it carefully before he signs. And don't forget your Notary Public kit. I want everything 'by the book' on this."

"Way ahead of you, Mr. C." Barbara patted her soft leather briefcase. "Got it right here."

"Good girl. Call me when you've handed the original to Nicholby."

"I'll call you from his office. Cheerio." She waved with a light-hearted flick of the hand and left us to our beers. As we sipped, I told Gus about my interviews with the Boardwalk Hall manager and with Sethwick. "I know Sethwick is hiding something," I insisted. "I just can't figure out what. He's involved in this murder somehow."

We heard the click of a door latch. Someone was in the outer office. Gus swung his feet off his desk and sat up straight, his face registering surprise. I turned my head in time to see Millie's complexion flash through several random shades of red. I stood. "I'll leave now, Gus."

"Sit down, Dick." Gus turned to Millie. "I think we should tell him."

Millie looked uncertain. "But we agreed."

"The situation's changed, Millie. Dick's been cleared."

This was like coming into a play midway through the second act. "Will someone please tell me what the hell is going on?"

Gus stood and pointed me back to my chair. "Sit down, Dick." He pointed to the chair next to mine. "You too, Millie." He took a sip of beer, then turned to Millie. "Want one?" She shook her head. "OK then. Dick," Gus continued as he sat back down behind his desk, "here's the story. Millie and I discussed your situation both before and after your arraignment. She was in the courtroom, remember?" He looked at me for confirmation and I nodded. "She was watching the Sutherland clan. And she also told me about Sethwick's visit to your office. Something about him bothered her."

Millie jumped in. "He didn't seem real, somehow. It was like a stage play. You know what I mean, Dick?" I nodded my agreement. The visit hadn't rung true to me either.

"Anyway," Gus continued, "Millie thought it might be useful for our team to have someone on the inside of the Sutherland empire. Under cover, so to speak. I agreed."

"Why keep it from me?"

"Because you would have tried to talk me out of it, Dick," Millie jumped in before Gus could answer. "Also, I figured I'd have a better chance of getting hired if the Sutherlands thought you and I were on the outs."

I was beginning to understand. "So you staged that scene at Happy's?"

Millie nodded. "It helped, too. I was asked about our relationship during my interview. I told them we were through, both personally and professionally. Happy corroborated my story completely."

"You used Happy as a reference?"

"He was a perfect character reference. We've know each other forever. We grew up on the same block and went to the same schools. He was two years ahead of me. Our families were friendly back then, too."

"Impressive." In truth, I thought it was pretty amazing. "You're a good actress, you know. You really had me fooled."

Millie chuckled. "You almost torpedoed me, though."

"I did? How?"

"When Sutherland's HR department called you for a work reference, you said I was 'damned good.' I had to do some slick verbal skating. They wondered why you gave me such a stellar referral." Millie laughed and so did I. It felt like coming home to share a laugh with her again. I raised my beer can in her direction. "Here's looking at you, kid," I said. Then I leaned over and kissed her gently on the forehead. "Thanks."

Twenty-one

Gus cleared his throat with a discrete 'ahem,' reminding us that he was in the room. "Enough of this," he said, smiling. "Millie, you came rushing in as though a division of demons was chasing you. What's up?"

"Well," she began, looking at Gus, "Dick's probably told you that he dropped in on Gordon Sethwick today." Gus nodded and Millie continued. "After Dick left, Sylvia Sutherland confronted her husband 'behind closed doors' in Mr. Sethwick's office. I was able to hear the first half of their conversation."

"How did you manage that?"

"There's an intercom on my desk that allows me to listen for a discrete message from the boss when there's someone with him. It's only supposed to be used under certain conditions - like if he wants to get rid of an unwanted guest politely, there's a key phrase he uses to signal me to buzz him with an urgent call. I simply flipped the intercom switch to the 'ON' position. I could hear everything."

"Were you able to record the conversation?" I asked.

"No, but I did the next best thing." Millie took a steno pad from her hand bag and held it up for us to see. "I took it all down in shorthand. Every word. Want to hear?"

"You bet!"

"Here goes." Millie flipped open her steno pad. "Sylvia Sutherland is S.S. and Gordon Sethwick is G.S.

"SS: 'What was he doing here?'

GS: 'He was asking questions.'

SS: 'About what?'

GS: 'The night of the ball. He was asking about the message - how it was delivered. He asked me why the messenger asked for me instead of Celine.'

SS: 'What did you tell him?'

GS: 'Just the bare bones. That the messenger gave me the envelope, and I gave it to Celine. I said I had no idea why the messenger asked for me.'

SS: 'What else?'

GS: 'He wanted to know what Celine did. How she reacted. So I told him.'

SS: 'And?'

GS: 'He wondered why I came to his office the Monday after the ball.'

SS: 'You didn't tell Dickens that I suggested you visit his office, I hope?'

GS: 'Of course not! I'm not a fool, Sylvia, whatever you may think. Besides, I had no desire to prolong the conversation.'

SS: 'Very well. I guess no harm was done. But you should have just called Security and had him ejected.'

GS: 'I'll keep that thought in mind for next time. Is that all, Sylvia?'

SS: 'No. There's one more thing. We might have a problem. Susan wants to meet with Barney and me. She's driving down from Burlington tomorrow.'

GS: 'What about?'"

Millie looked up from her notes. "That's all I was able to hear. The other secretaries were coming back in from lunch. The doors that separate the executive reception area from each executive secretary's office are always left open during business hours. It would have looked odd for me to have closed my door, and I couldn't take the chance of them catching me eavesdropping."

I sat quietly for a moment, digesting the information. "Gus," I said, "let's show Millie those notes."

"Sure, Dick."

He reached into a file folder that was sitting on his desk, extracted the four sheets of paper and handed them to me. I lined them up side by side in front of Millie. "Tell me what you see."

She glanced quickly over the four sheets, then looked at them again carefully. "Three of these are a series of drafts of the same message," she said, her voice thoughtful. "The fourth is different. I don't know who wrote the messages," she added, "but I can tell you one thing. All four notes look like they were typed on the same machine.

"We thought so, too," I told her. "But we don't know where or by whom."

She looked again at the notes. "I think I can tell you where," she said. "I think these were done on the IBM Selectric II typewriter that's on my desk at Sutherland's."

"Are you sure?"

"Pretty sure. See the defect in the upper case letter 'S'?" My golfball is the same type size - that smaller 'Elite' type that you hate, Dick - and it has the same defect."

"Who has access to the machine?"

"Each of the executive secretaries has her own typewriter on her desk, although I suppose any of them could have used mine before I came on the scene. The executives all have access, of course. Anyone with a key to the executive suite has access to all of our typewriters."

"Who has a key to the executive suite?"

135

"Each of the senior executives: that would be Sylvia Sutherland, Gordon Sethwick, and Mary Sue Thorpe, the head of HR. I assume that Celine Sutherland would have had a key, too. Oh, and I think the corporate attorney, Mr. Barnstable, has a key. He was the one who let me in this morning when I arrived early."

"The secretaries don't have keys?"

"No, I don't think so." She shook her head. "I haven't been given one, anyway; but, of course, I'm just a 'temp.' I believe Security has one, though. I heard one of the other girls say that there's always a security guard present when the cleaning staff does the executive suite."

"So at least five people have a key to the executive suite, including Sethwick, Sylvia, the HR head, Barnstable and the Security officer."

"That's right, Dick." Millie nodded. "And don't forget that the other secretaries would have access to my typewriter while I was at lunch or on an errand."

"Well," I said, "let's set that aspect aside for the moment. The first step is to confirm that these notes were typed on your machine. How do we do that?"

Millie thought for a moment. "We might be able to use the ribbon."

"The ribbon?"

"The typewriter ribbon cartridge. I'll check it tomorrow. I can drop by here after work, if that's OK with you, Gus."

"Millie," I objected, "I'm not so sure that's a good idea. Everyone knows Gus is my lawyer. Won't it look suspicious?"

Millie giggled, her eyes sparkling with mischief. "I'm afraid I haven't done your reputation any good, Dick. I've taken care to grouse about all the back pay you owe me. As far as the girls at the office know, I'm meeting with Gus to try and collect my money." With that, she stood, planted a kiss on the top of my head, waved a "too-de-loo" at Gus, and waltzed out of the office.

"That's some girl," Gus observed, with a smile.

"No, Gus." I shook my head slowly in admiration. "That's no girl. That's one helluva woman!"

Twenty two

Gus reached into his mini-fridge for a couple more beers. He handed me one, then reinstalled his unshod feet on his desk blotter. We sat and sipped, waiting for Barbara to call. The silence was warm and friendly, like the wool afghans my Grammy used to knit. I wrapped myself in it and let my mind wander. It roamed from Atlantic City to Everettville and back again; then to Sutherland's and beyond. When it reached Burlington, Vermont, I yanked its leash and sat straight up.

Gus looked up at me, one eyebrow cocked. "What is it, Dick?"

"Susan," I replied. "I'm worried."

"Why do you think she's coming to town?"

I shook my head. "I'm asking myself why Sylvia thinks that Susan's visit might pose a problem for her and Sethwick."

"I see what you mean." He paused. "You think she might be in danger?"

"Could be." I shifted in my seat. "Look, Gus, when Barbara calls, talk to Nicholby. Ask him to keep Bruno's statement and my status under wraps for now."

"You sure?"

I nodded. "Bruno's statement puts us a step closer to the killer. I don't want him or her to hear my footsteps yet. I want to let things continue to play out a while." I stood. "Thanks for everything, Gus."

"Where are you off to?"

"The public library. I want to catch up on the news." I turned to go just as the phone on Gus's desk started to ring. He picked up the receiver with one hand, while waving at me with the other. I could hear him saying, "Yes,

139

Barb. Now let me talk to Nicholby," as I closed his door behind me.

I left Gus's building and drove to the Atlantic City Free Public Library, located at the corner of Illinois and Pacific. I was lucky enough to find a parking spot right outside the Illinois Avenue main entrance. It was after six o'clock, so I didn't even need to feed the meter. The main library is an imposing three-story, gray granite structure that was completed in 1910 - thanks, in part, to one of Andrew Carnegie's many contributions to the arts and to literacy. It is surrounded by a perfectly manicured lawn, which is protected by a wrought iron fence just tall enough to discourage the development of random walking paths and deposits of dog droppings. The building's monolithic gray is softened by dark green ivy, which has spread like kudzu over at least one third of the facade.

I entered by the main door and headed for the reference librarian. In response to my question, she directed me to the file drawer that contained back issues of The Press. I plowed through the stack of papers and extracted all of the issues from Saturday, July 21ₛₜ forward. The Sunday paper devoted an entire color rotogravure section to photos and stories about the previous evening's Christmas in July ball. I studied the pictures. Sylvia Sutherland was featured prominently in most of them, some with Gordon Sethwick at her side, greeting guests as they arrived. Other photos showed Sylvia in the company of the state's most prominent citizens. There was a picture of Sethwick and the Governor opening the silent auction, and one of the Governor handing the gavel to Sylvia. I found a single photo of Celine, emerald-green evening bag held in her left hand, posing with Sylvia and Sethwick. Their body language shouted 'duty' pose. I used my pocket magnifying lens to examine Celine's evening bag, comparing it to the bag held in Sylvia's right hand. It was hard to be sure, but the bags looked identical in the photograph and neither one seemed to be bulging.

The Monday morning paper referred briefly to an unidentified body that was found on the beach near the Steel Pier the previous day. Police were investigating the 'suspicious death,' the paper advised its readers. The front section of Monday's evening edition was chock-full of stories about Celine's murder. My arrest was announced by the police in time to make the deadline for the Tuesday afternoon edition, and my arraignment earned a brief mention on Page 3 of the Wednesday evening paper. The report of Celine's funeral - held the afternoon of my arraignment - together with her obituary, filled an entire page of the Wednesday evening paper's Lifestyles section. I read through the report and obituary until I found what I was looking for; she was buried next to her mother in the Sutherland family plot at the Atlantic City Cemetery in Pleasantville.

There was an advertisement for the cemetery in one corner of the page containing the daily 'Hatch, Match and Dispatch' announcements. Office hours were 9-5; but the gates stayed open to visitors until 8:00pm. I checked my watch; it was just 7:15. I left the library and headed out to Pleasantville on US-40 and, after about 20 minutes, turned right on Doughty Road. The cemetery was on my right; I made a right turn, drove through the open gates, and followed the one-way perimeter road that meandered past the high rent district - the mausoleums and fenced-in family plots. At the far end of the cemetery, in a quiet corner away from all street noise, I spotted a wrought-iron fence with a sign that simply read 'Sutherland.'

I stopped behind a parked car, climbed out of my seat, and entered the Sutherland enclosure. In the dusk that had begun to envelop the cemetery, I saw a man, head bowed and shoulders shaking, standing at the foot of a fresh grave. He turned at the sound of my footsteps on the gravel path. It was Gordon Sethwick.

"You have your nerve," he greeted me, his voice quivering as he balled his hands into tight fists. "What do you mean by coming here?"

"I came to pay my respects to Celine," I replied, keeping my voice even.

"You have no right." His voice was low and strained; his entire body as clenched as his fists. "Get the hell out of here, you, you...murderer."

"I have as much right as you do," I retorted, stung into anger. "I did NOT kill Celine." I took a deep breath, then swallowed hard in a vain effort to calm down. "I intend to find out who did. I owe her that. And let me tell you something more, Mr. Gordon Sethwick." I walked over to him until we were nose to nose, and poked his chest with my finger as I bit off each word and spat it out. "If I find out that you were in any way responsible for Celine's death, I will nail your sorry ass to the nearest wall and let it hang there until the cops cut you down."

He jumped back at my vehemence, stared at me as though he had never seen me before, turned abruptly on his heel and left me alone. Alone with Celine and my thoughts.

Twenty-three

I stood at the side of a freshly dug grave and looked down at Celine as she stared back up at me from the bottom of the rectangular pit. She was dressed in her favorite outfit: faded jeans, a white T-shirt, and penny loafers on her otherwise bare feet. Her hair was drawn back into a ponytail and tied with a yellow ribbon. The same green pearl stud earrings that she was wearing when she first came to me for help were in her earlobes. "Help me, Damien," she said. "Find my killer. Protect my son."

I jerked awake. My heart was pounding and so was my head. The display on my clock radio read 03:27AM. But I was done sleeping. I could still see Celine's face and hear her voice. "Find my killer," I heard over and over in sync with the pounding. "Find my killer. Protect my son."

I got up and stood under the shower to wash away the remnants of the dream. Slowly, my heart rate returned to normal and the throbbing in my head softened to a tolerable level. I wrapped a towel around my waist, padded into the kitchen, and poured myself a tumbler of ice water. A couple of aspirins took care of the rest of my headache, but Celine's voice lingered still. "Protect my son. Find my killer."

"I'm trying, Celine," I whispered.

I rummaged through my kitchen cupboards until I found some real coffee, and set a pot to drip. While I was waiting, I retrieved Celine's autopsy report and the forensic lab report from the box of files that I had brought in from the car when I got home the night before, took a fresh pad of paper, and started to comb through the prosaic prose that is the backbone of all official reports. By the time my coffee was ready, I had already filled a sheet of paper with notes and queries. I carried on methodically, noting anything that was odd or unclear. I finished the pot of coffee and my review of the reports at about the same time.

It was just seven o'clock, and I felt wired from the combination of too little sleep and too much caffeine. Breakfast would help. My fridge was practically empty, but I found a couple of eggs that didn't smell of sulfur, and a heel of salami that hadn't yet grown whiskers. I diced up the salami and scrambled it with the eggs. A couple of slices of toast and jam completed the repast. I thought of making another pot of coffee, but settled for some milk that had just passed its 'Best If Used By' date instead.

The mountain of fat, cholesterol, and protein absorbed some of the excess caffeine, and I figured that it was now safe to shave without worrying about cutting my throat. By the time I was shaved, combed and dressed, it was after eight. I called the D.A.'s office and caught Nicholby as he was walking in the door. After the conventional pleasantries, we got down to business.

"What can I do for you, Dickens?" he asked.

"I'd like to visit with the Medical Examiner, and also with the head of Forensics," I paused to check my notes. "A guy named Bob Horton? I've been reviewing their reports and have some questions for them," I explained.

"No problem." I heard him rummaging for paper and a pen to scratch down a note. "Give me a few minutes to reach them. I'll advise both the M.E. and Horton to cooperate with you. If you don't hear back from me in the next five minutes, plan on 9:00am for Dr. Meecham, then hit the Forensics lab after that."

I remembered Dr. Meecham's name from the autopsy report. I thanked Nicholby, transferred my pad of notes into my 'going visiting' briefcase, then gave Gus a call to let him know what I was up to. I refreshed my memory on the location of the Medical Examiner's office - the county had moved the department to a new facility a year or so before - checked a map, and steered my Celica back onto

US-40. I turned left on South Main, which changed its name to Shore Road when I reached the city limits of Northfield.

The Medical Examiner's office is part of the Atlantic County Department of Public Safety. It's housed in a converted warehouse - a single-story white structure set at the back of a complex of several three-story red brick office buildings. The utilitarian landscaping - faded grass punctuated by a few trees and some tired shrubs - screamed 'government issue.' I followed the signs to the main entrance and walked up to the reception desk just as the digital wall clock display behind the desk changed to 09:00.

While I waited for the receptionist to locate Dr. Meecham, I studied the public service posters that exhorted me to 'Say No To Drugs,' to 'Name a Designated Driver' when partying, and to 'Obey the Speed Limits.' As befitted a county that is home to one of the nation's largest cigarette manufacturers, 'No Smoking' posters were not part of the collection. I was so intent on the display that I nearly jumped out of my skin when a brisk female voice behind me asked, "Mr. Dickens?" I turned to see a woman looking up at me from a 5'4" frame, her right hand extended in greeting. "Natalie Meecham," she said. "George Nicholby told me to expect you." I shook her hand. Her grip was firm, her hand cool. Her white lab coat was starched and professional, as was her manner.

"Damien Dickens," I responded. "Thanks for seeing me on short notice."

She nodded and pointed down the corridor. "Let's go to my office," she said. "We can talk there." She wheeled and set a brisk pace down the long, institutional gray hallway. She had a head start, and I was hard-pressed to catch up to her. About halfway down the hall, she turned and motioned me into a cubbyhole. The furnishings were spartan: steel double-pedestal desk with filing cabinet to

145

match, a steel-frame swivel desk chair, minimally padded on the back, seat and arms, and one matching 'guest' chair. Meecham's medical diplomas provided the only wall decoration. I glanced out the one small window, which overlooked a loading dock; a County Coroner's ambulance was in the process of making a delivery. Dr. Meecham motioned me to the chair and we both sat.

We appraised each other silently across her painfully tidy desk. She leaned slightly forward, her clasped hands resting on the desk blotter in a pose that reminded me of Miss Bowles, my fifth grade teacher. Her hair had once been dark brown - perhaps chestnut - but was now flecked with gray, giving it a 'salt and pepper' look. Her eyes were steel blue, with dark flecks. Laugh lines and a few wrinkles on her forehead and around the corners of her mouth gave character to an otherwise plain face. I placed her age as fifty-ish. "How can I be of help?" she asked.

"I assume George Nicholby told you that I have some questions relating to the autopsy report on Celine Sutherland?"

"Yes, he told me that much," She nodded and pulled a file towards her. I decided to plunge right in.

"What can you tell me about the wound?"

"It was caused by a single shot to the chest at close range. It's all in the report," she said, her voice as brisk as her manner as she tapped the manila folder with her index finger.

"No chance there were two shots?"

"No."

"You're sure?"

"Look," she snapped. "If all you're doing is fishing, then this is a waste of time." She looked at her watch. "Now, if you'll excuse me, I have an autopsy scheduled."

"I'm sure the patient won't mind waiting."

146

"Mister Dickens." She stood, her voice and body quivering with suppressed indignation. "I'll thank you to leave. I don't take kindly to that sort of flippancy."

She was right, of course. "I apologize, Doctor," I said. "Please. Can you give me just a few more minutes? There's something else I'd like to clarify in my mind."

She took a deep breath and sat back down. "Very well."

"The close-up photos of the face show some discoloration around the nose and mouth."

"Yes?"

"Your report describes them as chemical burns."

She flipped through a couple of pages in the file, then nodded. "That's right. I noted that on page 4 of the report."

"Can you speculate on when the burns occurred or what may have caused them?"

"Well," she said, "I'd guess they were fairly recent - they hadn't formed scabs. Any number of chemicals might have caused that type of injury."

"Could she have been chloroformed? Might that have caused the burns?"

She thought for a moment, then nodded. "If the chloroform was in contact with her skin for several minutes, it might have caused a burn."

"What if a chloroform-soaked cloth was pressed up against her face and tied in place?"

She opened her drawer, took out a large magnifying lens, and examined the close-up photo of Celine's face carefully. "It's possible." She handed me the magnifier and turned the photo toward me. "Look closely at the corners of her mouth," she said. "There are tiny marks that might have been caused by a cord or scarf tied tightly around her

147

mouth. It could have been holding a cloth soaked with chloroform in place."

"Would the chloroform have left any traces in her blood or tissues that the lab work would have picked up?"

"Unlikely." She shook her head. "We ran the standard toxicology panel on her blood and organs. It doesn't include chloroform though. A negative result wouldn't have meant much, anyway. Chloroform is such a volatile chemical that it clears from the blood and tissues very quickly. She was killed several hours before her body was found. Chances of finding traces of chloroform in her blood or organs by the time I received the body for autopsy would have been just about nil."

She looked at her watch again and stood. "I really must go," she said. "If you have any other questions, please call me and we'll set up another appointment."

I rose and extended my hand. "Thank you for your time," I said. "This has been a big help."

"I'll walk you to the door," she offered.

I hesitated a moment. "Just one last thing?"

"What?" She stopped, one hand on the door knob.

"Could you tell from the nature of the wound how quickly she died?"

"The bullet went right through her heart. Death would have been virtually instantaneous."

"So she didn't suffer?"

"No, Mr. Dickens." Dr. Meecham's voice and eyes softened as she looked up at me. "She didn't suffer."

Twenty-four

I drove back into Atlantic City to keep my appointment with Bob Horton. The forensics lab is housed in the basement of police headquarters. As much as I would have preferred to give the place a wide berth, that's where I was heading. At least this time, I'd be walking in through the front door. I arrived at the red brick building on Atlantic Ave. between California and Iowa at about 10:30. I'd never met Bob Horton, who had recently transferred over to the ACPD from the State lab, and I hadn't yet decided whether to show the pop bottles to him, or simply to turn them over to the D.A. But I grabbed the plastic bag containing the bottles from the trunk of my car and brought it inside with me, just in case. I gave my name to Sgt. Donna Mickelburg, the officer on duty, and asked to see the head of Forensics. "Thought you'd never want to see this place again, Dickens," she commented, eyeballing me. "Is Mr. Horton expecting you?"

I assured Mickelburg that I was expected, and sat down to wait, avoiding eye contact with the row of pimps seated on the benches lined up against the wall, waiting to bail out their girls. I found a seat at the end of a bench, next to one of the less disreputable looking characters, leaned my back against the wall, and folded my arms to wait.

The guy beside me - his name was Lenny, he volunteered - turned to me. "Don't remember seeing you here before," he said. "You new in town?"

I shook my head. He elbowed me to get my attention. "One of your girls busted?"

"I'm in a different trade," I replied. "Just waiting to see someone."

"Mouthpiece, then?"

149

I shook my head again. I really didn't feel like exchanging confidences with this mug.

"Okay, okay." He threw up his hands, palms out. "I give up. Just trying to make polite conversation. Pass the time, like."

To my relief, I heard my name called. I walked over to the desk, where Sgt. Mickelburg had me sign the register before she clipped a Visitor badge to my breast pocket. She buzzed me through the gate and made perfunctory introductions. Bob Horton nodded an acknowledgement and motioned me down a long, narrow corridor. We went through a doorway at the far end of the hall and down a flight of stairs to the basement. The stairwell opened into yet another long, narrow hall, lit poorly with flickering fluorescent fixtures.

Horton led me to the second door on the left, and ushered me into a small office. "We can talk in here," he said, as he waved me toward a seat. His office was the size of a large janitor's closet. It was sparsely furnished, which was a good thing, as there was barely enough space for the desk, two chairs and narrow filing cabinet. There was no bookcase - just a couple of wood-plank shelves clinging to one wall with the aid of metal brackets. The planks were bowed in the center from the weight of the reference books they held, the shelving taking up nearly half the length of the wall. Opposite the bookshelves was a door that led directly from the office into the lab. A window in the upper portion of the door allowed Horton to keep an eye on the lab staff from his office. A stack of overstuffed manila folders teetered on the corner of his desk, and a single file folder rested on the desk blotter.

"Cozy set-up," I commented, as I settled into my unpadded wood chair.

"It's small," he acknowledged with a shrug, "but it does the job. I spend most of my time in the lab, anyway."

We sat and stared at each other for a long moment. "I understand you have some questions about the Sutherland case?" he said at last.

"That's right." I reached into my pocket and pulled out my notes. "I was reading the ballistics report, and something seemed to be missing," I began.

"Missing?" He bridled slightly. "What are you suggesting is missing?"

"Well, whenever I've seen these reports in the past, there's a verbal description, and photos of the condition of the bullet before it was cleaned for microscopy." He nodded. "But I didn't see anything like that in the Sutherland ballistics report."

"That's because the bullet came to us clean."

"No blood residue?"

He shook his head.

"No tissue?" I persisted. "No bits of bone or threads of fabric from her clothes?"

"Nope."

"Clean as a whistle, then?"

"That's right - just a couple of wood splinters from its final resting place in the Boardwalk fascia." He opened the file folder that lay in front of him, and flipped through several pages before turning the folder around for me to see. "There's the description of the splinters," he said, pointing me to a spot halfway down the page.

"Isn't that unusual?"

He shrugged. "It is what it is. If we had found anything else on the bullet, we would have logged it."

"How clear was the pattern on the slug?"

"Clear enough to tell that it was fired from the gun found at the scene. Your gun," he added with a scowl, "if memory serves me." Horton stood and opened the connecting door to the lab. "Come on in, if you like. I'll show you the slug and the test results."

Three people glanced up from their lab benches as we entered the room. The lighting, in a feeble attempt to providing an ergonomic work environment, was supplied by daylight fluorescent tubes. In the slightly pink flickering light, the lab denizens reminded me of Morlocks - the underground post-nuclear race of beings in H.G. Wells's classic, The Time Machine. We walked over to a locked cabinet. Horton pulled out a key ring, selected a key, and opened the second drawer from the top. He took out a small box labeled "Sutherland. Case #1979-175-1" and beckoned me over to a two-headed microscope. He sat down at the microscope, removed two slugs from the evidence box, and placed them side by side on the stage. After fiddling with the focus wheels, he invited me to peer through the second set of eyepieces.

"The slug on the left was test-fired from the Smith & Wesson Model 29 found at the scene; the right-hand slug was pried out of the Boardwalk fascia," he explained. "There is no doubt that both slugs were fired from the same gun. The striation patterns don't lie." I stared through the microscope at the pattern of lines - the ballistic equivalent of fingerprints - on the two slugs. They were virtually identical. The gun found at the scene - my gun - had fired both bullets. Horton cleared his throat and started to fidget. I took the hint and stood. He retrieved the slugs from the microscope stage, returned them to their box, and locked the box back into the cabinet. "Was there anything else?" he asked.

I shook my head. "Not right now. Can I call you if something comes to mind?"

He nodded and fished a card out of his shirt pocket. "My direct line number is on this. An answering machine will pick up if I'm not at my desk." He ushered me back out into the hallway. As we started walking toward the stairs, I heard footsteps behind me, then felt a hand clamp down hard on my left shoulder. I whirled around and came face to face with Lt. Holmes.

"You." He pointed his finger in my face, then jerked his thumb in the direction of a door marked 'Authorized Personnel Only.' "In there." I hesitated. "Now!" Holmes opened the door and flipped on the light switch. The room was the size of a janitor's closet, just like Horton's office. Except that this room really was a janitor's closet. Mops leaned against one wall, the mop heads suspended over yawning buckets. Cleaning supplies filled the shelves that lined the opposite wall. I found myself wondering what Holmes had in mind. Was he planning on sic'ing Mickey Mouse in the guise of The Sorcerer's Apprentice on me in an effort to soak a confession out of me? A sour taste of resentment seethed up into my throat at the unfairness of the situation. I'd been cleared, but Holmes didn't know it. I turned to vent my anger and frustration at him. But the impulse died when I saw his right hand extend towards me, a look of contrition on his face.

"Truce?" he asked.

"I guess." My response was wary, even as I took his hand to shake on the cease-fire he was offering. I wasn't sure what was going on.

"I just got off the phone with the D.A.," Holmes said by way of explanation. "The Department owes you an apology." He took a breath, then muttered, "And so do I."

I managed a smile and a shrug. "It's OK, Lieutenant." I thought for a moment and added, "I hope Nicholby told you I wanted this kept quiet for now."

"Yeah." He smiled self-consciously - Holmes wasn't an easy smiler. "That's why I dragged you into this closet. This isn't my regular office, you know." He chuckled briefly, then got down to business. "The D.A. said that you had a few questions about the case, and a couple of ideas. Anything you care to share?"

"Well, I still have more questions than answers," I hedged. I wasn't quite ready to reveal everything I suspected. "Let's pull up a couple of pails and talk."

We inspected the bottoms of several buckets, and found two that looked sturdy enough and clean enough to sit on. "Here's where I'm at," I said. "Someone has gone through a lot of effort to frame me, and has put multiple layers of insulation between Celine's murder and himself." I paused, then added, "Or herself."

"Go on," he nodded.

"The outermost layer was Benny Caravaggio." I held up one finger. "He's dead. The second layer was Bruno Caravaggio, Benny's nephew." I held up a second finger. "He survived through sheer dumb luck. Bruno was hired by a biker named Cosmo. I think Cosmo is the one who killed Benny." I held up a third finger. "I don't know who hired Cosmo, but that makes at least three layers of protection for whoever orchestrated this death waltz."

"What else have you found out?"

"Celine Sutherland died from a single bullet wound to the heart, according to the M.E. And only one bullet was recovered at the scene. A clean slug - no blood or tissue on it."

"So?"

"So, I found these at the scene." I opened the plastic bag that I had been carrying around with me and showed the bottles to Holmes. "They were under the Boardwalk near where Celine's body was discovered. I think they were used as silencers. I also found another note, which my attorney showed Nicholby yesterday morning."

Holmes removed a tissue from his pocket and used it to pick up one of the bottles, tilting it this way and that to examine it. "Go on."

"OK," I told him. "Here's how I think the hit went down. Celine was lured out of the ballroom by a fake note threatening her son. She was waylaid, perhaps in the parking lot on the way to her car. I presume that her car was still in the Boardwalk Hall parking lot after her body was found?" Holmes nodded confirmation, and I continued. "I believe that she was chloroformed to knock her out, then gagged with a chloroform-soaked cloth to keep her unconscious (the M.E. agrees that she may have been, by the way). The perps - there needed to be two people to handle this - shoved her into a car and drove to the area of the Steel Pier. Then they carried Celine onto the beach, where she was laid down on the sand partway under the Boardwalk and shot, after which they removed the gag. The bullet went through her body and probably buried itself in the sand. You might want to dig for it. Once Celine was taken care of, one of the perps slugged me from behind and lifted my gun and wallet. A single shot was fired from my weapon directly into the wood fascia of the Boardwalk so that your men would find a slug to match my gun and tie the killing to me."

Holmes stared at me, his eyes thoughtful. "What do you have to back up this theory?"

"Just these bottles and the note I found under the Boardwalk," I acknowledged. "Also the fact that the slug your people retrieved from the fascia was squeaky clean - no blood or tissue residue. You've got to admit that's unusual."

Holmes stood and rubbed his backside, grimacing. "These bucket seats would never make it in Detroit." He took the plastic bag from me and put the bottles back inside. "I'll give these to Horton; have him dust them for prints and measure the calibre of the holes. And I'll send my team back to the beach to look for that second slug," he promised. "Is there anything else you can think of?"

"Yeah." I stood and massaged a few sore spots. "Find this guy Cosmo. The Everettville cops probably have a decent description by now." I thought for a minute. "And protect Bruno Caravaggio. His mother, too. Bruno's our only link to the killing. Besides, I like the kid, now that he's come clean."

"I'll double the guard on him until this is done," Holmes promised. "Let me know if you turn up anything else." He handed me a card and wrote the phone number for the direct line to his office on the back. We shook hands again, and Holmes walked me out to the front desk, his right hand gripping my left arm. "Get the hell out of here, Dickens," he growled, as he turned away.

I signed the register and handed my Visitor badge back to the desk sergeant with a shrug, waved a jaunty farewell to Lenny the pimp, and breezed out the door. I had just passed 'GO' and earned a 'Get Out Of Jail Free' card from 'Community Chest' in a single throw of the dice.

Twenty-five

My stomach was telling me that it was time for lunch, so I jaywalked across Atlantic Avenue and entered junk food heaven, otherwise known as Josie's Diner. I hadn't been inside Josie's since I'd left the ACPD, but the menu hadn't changed. Except for the prices, of course; the BLT was now a buck ninety-five. I ordered one for old times' sake, along with a side of fries. Just to make sure that I had all the essential food groups covered, I added a strawberry shake to wash everything down.

After using my straw to vacuum up the last drop of the shake to the accompaniment of rude sucking sounds, I decided to leave my car in the police lot's free parking zone and walk over to the hospital to check on Bruno. I figured that the twelve block walk would be appropriate penance for my lunchtime indulgence. I approached the hospital just in time to see a tall, burly black man wearing a black leather jacket emerge from the revolving entry door and stride rapidly over to the motorcycle parking area. I broke into a run, but I was too far away. Before I could reach the parking lot, he had donned a white crash helmet emblazoned with gold lightning bolts, kick-started his bike, and roared off, leaving gravel, dirt, and something shiny in his wake. He had to stop for some incoming traffic, which allowed me to close the gap, but all I got for my pains was a face full of motorcycle exhaust fumes and the last two digits of a filthy license plate. As I trotted back toward the hospital entrance, I spotted a cigarette lighter wallowing in a fresh blob of grease. I fished a clean tissue from my pocket and bent down to retrieve the object, which had cartwheeled along the pavement as the motorbike accelerated through the parking lot. It was a 14K gold Dunhill with a monogram etched into one side, the second letter of which was a delicately filagreed 'S'. The first letter of the monogram was obscured by grease and dirt. I wrapped the lighter gently in several layers of tissue, put the wad in my trousers pocket, and trotted into the hospital lobby. Once inside, I grabbed the nearest pay phone and dialed Holmes on his direct line. "This is Dickens." I stopped briefly to cough out some residual bike exhaust. "I'm in the hospital lobby. I think I just spotted Cosmo leaving."

"Cosmo?"

"Yeah. The guy who recruited Bruno. He's driving a Harley. Wearing a black leather jacket and a white helmet with gold lightning bolts."

"Did you get the plate number?"

"Just the last two digits. Seven-seven. And something else. He dropped a 14K gold Dunhill lighter in the parking lot. It has a monogram on it. Look, I gotta go and check on Bruno. I'll drop off the lighter as soon as I can." I heard Holmes promise to 'get right on it' as I hung up.

I raced up the main staircase to the second floor, taking the steps two at a time, and turned right when I reached the top of the stairs. The hallway was empty; not a cop in sight, and the chair outside the door to Bruno's room had disappeared. My heart pounding, I raced down the hall and peered through the open doorway of his room. Bruno was gone. In his place was a petite white-haired woman, propped up on pillows, watching TV. She turned her head toward me as I burst in on her.

"How nice," she chirped with a smile. "Another visitor." She pointed to a straight-backed chair beside her bed. "I'm Mrs. Ida Pfeifferham. What's your name, young man?"

"Damien Dickens," I panted.

"I'm so pleased to meet you. Won't you sit down?" She gestured again to the chair.

"Wha... whe.... where is he?"

"Where's who, dear?"

"Bruno. Where's Bruno?" I was stammering, laboring under a twin disadvantage of confusion and anxiety.

She looked at me, puzzled. "You mean that large man who burst into the room and didn't even stay to visit?"

"No." I took a deep breath and exhaled slowly. "I mean the man whose room this is. Or was."

"Well, I don't know, dear." She moved her shoulders up and down in a delicate shrug. "They just moved me in here an hour or so ago. Interrupted my favorite soap opera, too. Very inconsiderate of them, wouldn't you say?" She smiled gently, and the skin around her china blue eyes crinkled. She had kind eyes.

"Very inconsiderate." I smiled in return and started to back out of the room. "Sorry I disturbed you."

"Not at all, dear," she replied with a little wave. "I hope you find your Bruno."

"So do I," I muttered as I headed for the nurses' station. "So do I."

The station was deserted. I waited impatiently, shifting my weight from foot to foot and checking my watch every fifteen seconds. At last, I saw a white-clad figure marching toward me from the far end of the hall. I hadn't seen this nurse before. Her uniform was starched so thoroughly that I could hear it crackling from twenty yards away. Her bearing was as stiff as her uniform, and her prow would have done credit to the USS Missouri. White support hose and a pair of white oxfords completed her ensemble. When she reached the nurses' station, I could see that her face was round, and was framed by a disciplined shock of curly gray hair. A traditional nurse's cap - white with one thin, blood-red stripe - crowned her head, and a set of steel-rimmed reading glasses hung from her neck, resting on her bosom. A pin affixed to her left breast pocket proclaimed her to be Miss Beasley.

"Yes?" Her manner was as stiff as her uniform.

159

"I'm looking for Bruno Caravaggio."

"Are you a relative?"

"No. A friend."

"We can't give out any information, except to immediate family." She glanced at her wristwatch. "If you'll excuse me, I have rounds to complete."

"Wait." I put my hand on her arm to restrain her. "He was on this floor yesterday. I visited him." I pointed to his old room. "In that room." She hesitated. "Look," I fished a business card out of my wallet. "My name is Damien Dickens. I'm a private investigator. I know he's under police protection. I'm on the list of people allowed to visit."

"Do you have some I.D.?"

I handed her my driver's license, and she made a call. She repeated my name, spelling it for the person on the other end of the line, nodded and returned the receiver to its cradle.

"OK, Mr. Dickens," She handed me back my license. "Take the elevator to the fifth floor. Someone will meet you there."

A young uniformed cop holding a clipboard greeted me as I stepped out of the elevator. A sign on the wall over his head proclaimed this floor to be 'The Arthur Sutherland Wing'. The constable checked my ID against his list, gave me a pat-down, and escorted me down the hall. I could see two more uniformed officers in the hallway - one at the door to the stairwell at the far end of the hall, and one standing post outside Bruno's room.

"Hey, Pop." Bruno greeted me with a cheerful wave as I stuck my head inside his room. "What do you think of my new digs?"

I looked around. This was the Ritz of hospital rooms. The walls were wainscoted at waist height, with chintz wallpaper in earth tones below and matching paint - a pleasing pastel burnt umber - above. The floor was covered with 16" square beige travertine tiles laid on the diagonal, with a border of 6" square travertine tiles in shades of medium to dark burnt umber around the perimeter. The room had a separate sitting area, which was furnished with an upholstered sofa large enough to seat three people comfortably, two matching armchairs, a walnut coffee table, and a matching lamp table at one end of the sofa. A floor lamp stood in dignified solitude in the corner. A low walnut stand supported one of the largest television sets I'd ever seen, and a second TV hung on the wall opposite Bruno's bed.

"Not bad, Bruno." I smiled and nodded. "How did you swing this?"

"Orders from headquarters." He indicated a chair near his bed. "Have a seat, Pop." He waited for me to make myself comfortable, then continued. "Extra cops turned up about an hour ago. They had me moved up here."

"Nice." I looked around again as a stray thought struck me. "Hope you don't get stuck with the tab."

He laughed, then winced. "Still hurts a bit to laugh. Cops are paying."

"Where's Sophia?"

"Mom's at the pawnshop. She's taking care of it until I take over."

"Are you sure that's a good idea?"

"She insisted. Now that I'm on the mend, she said that she needed to be doing something useful." He sensed my concern and added, "Two cops are staying with her. One's a lady cop - stays with her all night in Benny's old apartment back of the shop. The other one's a guy - stays out front of the shop 24/7."

"That's good." I felt a bit better knowing that Holmes had taken care of business. "I think Cosmo tried to get to you just before I arrived. I notified the cops. If we're lucky, they'll pick him up."

"Is Mom in danger?" He sat bolt upright, his face compressing suddenly in reaction to the pain triggered by his abrupt movement. He gasped, then started to swing his legs over the side of the bed.

"Sounds like she's well protected. Get back into bed, you idiot." I lifted his legs up and rolled him back into bed, none too gently."I'll swing by the shop and check on her."

"Thanks, Pop." He laid back down, breathing heavily, his pajamas damp with sweat. "I swear, I can't even sit up without the room spinning."

"Take it easy, kid." I waved as I left the room. "I'll drop in again tomorrow."

I walked back to police headquarters to drop off the Dunhill and pick up my car. I stood in line at the desk sergeant's counter. My old friend Lenny was just ahead of me, and we exchanged greetings. Lt. Holmes was in a meeting, Sgt. Mickelburg informed me when I reached the head of the line. I asked her to let him know that I had dropped by, and would be back later that day. "Is it true, Dickens?" Mickelburg whispered as I turned to leave.

"Is what true?"

"That you've been cleared in the Sutherland murder," she persisted. "A rumor started making the rounds shortly after you left here."

"No comment," I replied with a wink and a wave as I headed for the door.

I retrieved my car from the parking lot behind police headquarters and drove to Benny's pawn shop. I had a word with the cop standing post before going in to see Sophia. She'd clearly been hard at work. Every surface had been scrubbed, the brass musical instruments were gleaming, and all the silver on display was freshly polished. Everything was dusted to perfection, and the floor swept clean. The only jarring note was a pristine 4' x 8' sheet of plywood that filled a gaping hole where the plate glass window used to be. Sophia was standing at the counter, drawing something on a large sheet of paper. She looked up with a welcoming smile. "What do you think?" She swept her arm in a 180° arc to encompass the shop. "I have a new display window on order. It should be installed next week."

"Looks like a different place. Spiffy. Must have been a pile of work for you."

"It's all for Bruno." She cocked her head and smiled. "You know that Benny left him the shop?" I nodded.

"What do you think of this?" She turned the sheet of paper around for me to look at. "I'm working on some ads. I was a graphic arts major in college. I'm a bit rusty, but…"

"It looks great, Sophia." I heard a bell ring as the front door opened and a woman walked in with a young girl in tow. "I think you have a customer. I'd better let you get back to work."

Twenty-six

I had been avoiding my office as much as possible - it was just too empty without Millie - but I'd wimped out long enough. I had some time before my late afternoon date with Gus. Enough time to deal with my mail, anyway. I settled at my desk and sifted through the accumulated stacks of bills, ads, magazines, and solicitations for various charities. I had just finished tossing the junk and was sorting the bills into piles labeled 'pay now,' 'pay later,' and 'screw 'em' when I was saved by the bell.

I grabbed the phone on the first ring. "Dickens."

"Lieutenant Holmes here. We've got Cosmo in custody."

"Great! That's fast work." I could feel a pool of tension seep out from between my shoulder blades. "How did you find him so quickly?"

"We got lucky. A rookie traffic officer was a bit overzealous." I could hear Holmes blush through the phone. "She stopped his bike for a dirty license plate. When she ran his permit and plate number, the APB popped up and she made the arrest."

"So what happens now?"

"For the moment, we're holding him for conspiracy to defraud, based on Bruno Caravaggio's statement. Hang on." He put his hand over the mouthpiece, and I could hear muffled conversation oozing through between his fingers. "OK. Sorry. The judge just cut us a search warrant for Cosmo's apartment, and for the place where he garages his bike. Sgt. Sherlock is on his way with a forensics team to execute the search."

I groaned internally at the thought of ham-handed Sherlock in charge of the search, but kept my trap diplomatically shut. "Any chance of linking Cosmo -

165

what's the guy's last name, by the way - to Benny's murder?"

"Poindexter. His name is Tiberias Poindexter." Holmes barked a short laugh. "Cosmo is his 'handle' in the biker community. I have a call in for the Everettville sheriff. We'll try to get that witness down here tomorrow to look at a line-up." He paused, and I could hear more voices in the background. "Look, Dickens, I've gotta go. I'll keep you posted."

My hands were damp with relief; I reached into my pocket for a tissue to dry them, and encountered something hard. I removed the Dunhill from my pocket, rescued it from the wad of tissue in which I had wrapped it, placed it on my desk blotter and stared at the grease-covered insignia. Should I or shouldn't I? If I wiped off the grease and grime, I would obliterate any fingerprints. On the other hand, would fingerprints even have survived the grease bath? 'Probably not,' a little devil whispered in my left ear. 'You'll be destroying evidence,' riposted my good angel. I gazed at the lighter for a while, then rewrapped it carefully, placed it in a clean envelope, slid the package into my pocket, and headed for the door before I changed my mind. I'd swing by police headquarters before going over to see Gus.

I walked into the reception area and noticed the usual bench populated with the usual scum. This place was becoming more familiar to me than my own office. I stood in line and waited for Sgt. Mickelburg to finish with the pimp who was ahead of me, then asked to see Lt. Holmes. Mickelburg motioned for me to take a seat. "He might be tied up with an interrogation. Let me check."

Holmes appeared a few minutes later, looking impatient. "What is it, Dickens? I'm crowded for time."

I held out the envelope. "I think you'll be interested in this."

He hefted the envelope. "The lighter?" Holmes turned on his heel and motioned me to follow him. He led me down the hall and up one flight of stairs to his office. He cleared a space on his desk by moving a stack of papers onto the corner of a book-laden credenza, and centered the envelope carefully on his blotter. "Tell me again how you found this," he ordered as he unwrapped the package as though it was worth its weight in gold - which it was.

I recited in detail the events that took place outside the hospital, beginning with when I spotted Cosmo, and ending with my finding the lighter in a grease puddle.

"Are you sure it's Cosmo's?"

"Well, I saw something fly away from the bike as he peeled off. I can't be 100% certain," I admitted, "but my hunch is that it fell out of his pocket when he gunned the bike. I found it when I retraced the bike's track through the hospital parking lot."

Holmes flicked the switch labeled 'Forensics' on his intercom. "Horton, I need you in my office. Pronto." He released the switch without waiting for a reply. We stood and stared at the lighter while Bob Horton ascended from his basement bailiwick to the rarified atmosphere of the second floor. He arrived after a few minutes, panting slightly.

"Sorry I took so long." Horton stopped and caught his breath, doing a double-take when he saw me standing across the desk from Holmes. "Damned elevator was stuck on five, so I took the stairs." He hesitated briefly, no doubt wondering whether or not to acknowledge my presence.

Holmes waved Horton over to his desk. "I want you to have a look at this thing Dickens just brought in. What are the chances of picking up any latent prints on it?"

Horton stared at the lighter from all angles, then pulled a large tweezer with rubberized tips from his breast pocket and looked at Holmes. "May I?" Without waiting for a reply, he used the tweezer to flip the lighter over. He issued a few 'tut-tuts,' shaking his head several times. Finally, he stood erect and replaced the tweezer in his pocket. "Not a chance. Not with all that grease."

Holmes nodded. "Then we might as well clean the thing and see if there are any identifying marks. According to Dickens, there's a monogram that could tell us something."

Horton reached into his trouser pocket and took out a hinged box about the size of a flip-top cigarette package. He opened the box and extracted a bottle of liquid and a soft cloth. Then he proceeded to clean away the grease as carefully as an archeologist handling a 10,000-year old artifact. After a few minutes, he placed the clean lighter back on the desk, with the monogram face up. We stared at it in silence, then Horton cleared his throat.

"I think the second letter is 'S'. What do you think, Lieutenant?"

"I agree. How about you, Dickens?"

I made it unanimous. I had seen enough of the monogram to make out the 'S' even when it was still smeared with grease. "What about the first initial?"

Horton pulled out a magnifying lens and squinted at the monogram. "Might be a 'G' - or maybe a 'C' with a scratch in it. Hard to tell." He passed the lens to Holmes, who tilted the lighter through various angles, trying to decide. "C. I think it's a C," Holmes pronounced.

I held out my hand. "Mind if I look?"

Holmes handed me the lens. "Help yourself."

I went through the same contortions. "I don't know. Looks more like a G to me."

Holmes shook his head. "I think you're wrong, Dickens. It's a C. The monogram is C.S." He rapped the surface of his desk twice for emphasis. "C.S.," he repeated.

"Celine Sutherland. That punk probably took the lighter from her bag after he killed her." He grabbed the Dunhill, flung a crisp "Come with me" to me over his shoulder, and strode out of the office without waiting to see whether or not I was following him.

I trotted after Holmes, catching up to him as he approached the interrogation room. I grabbed him by the arm, and he turned to face me. "You're wrong about the monogram," I told him.

He said nothing, just opened a door and gestured me inside. We were in an observation room, and I could see Cosmo through the one-way glass, glaring silently at Sgt. Sherlock, while another uniformed officer stood, arms folded, leaning against the wall. "Is that the guy you saw leaving the hospital?" Holmes asked me.

I nodded. There was a wall phone in the room. Holmes picked up the receiver, and I could see Sherlock doing likewise. "Come in here a minute," Holmes ordered. I saw Sherlock say something to the other officer and walk out the door. He entered the observation room and looked back and forth between Holmes and me, a puzzled expression on his face that was a joy to behold.

"Dickens here has ID'd the prisoner as the person he saw in the hospital parking lot," Holmes explained as he handed the lighter to Sherlock. "Take this. Show it to Cosmo, and make sure he sees the monogram. We think..." He paused and corrected himself. "I think that he lifted it from the victim's handbag. Dickens isn't so sure."

Sherlock turned the lighter over in his hands, examining it. "Nice." He held it up. "You want I should add it to the evidence locker?"

"No. Bring it back to me here when you're done."

We watched Sherlock stroll back into the interrogation room, tossing the lighter in the air and catching it as he walked over to the table. "Look what I found, Poindexter," he said, placing the lighter on the table. "Recognize it?"

"Hey, where'd you get this?" Cosmo reached for the lighter, but Sherlock was there first.

"Not so fast." He gripped Cosmo's wrist. "Who'd you lift this from?"

"I never stole it. It was a gift."

"Pull the other leg, Poindexter," Sherlock snorted. "It's got bells on."

"I swear." Cosmo was staring at the lighter. "A guy gave it to me."

Sherlock picked up the lighter and started tossing it in the air again. "Make me believe that some guy would give the likes of you a solid gold Dunhill with a monogram on it. Especially when the monogram doesn't match any of your aliases."

"It's true," Cosmo insisted. "I met this guy in the alley behind the Imperial to transact some business. He offered me a smoke and pulled out the Dunhill to light my cigarette. I said something like 'nice Bic' and he offered it to me."

"Just like that."

"Yeah, just like that."

"No strings?"

"Well, I guess he considered it a bonus for the job I was doing."

"And what job was that?"

Cosmo shrugged wordlessly.

"What did this guy look like, then?"

"Hard to say. It was dark in the alley, and he wore a hat down low over his eyes. But he was tall."

"What was his name?"

"He never told me. He said to call him Mr. G"

Holmes picked up the receiver and pressed a button on the wall phone. "I've heard enough," he told Sherlock when the sergeant answered his buzz. "Bring back the lighter, then warehouse him 'til morning."

Sherlock returned the lighter, then left us alone. "How did you guess?" Holmes asked.

"Celine Sutherland didn't smoke." I stopped and thought a moment, then added. "But Gordon Sethwick does."

Twenty-seven

I retrieved the lighter, took my leave of Holmes, and headed for Gus's office. When I arrived, Millie was already installed in one of the upholstered client chairs, an IBM typewriter ribbon cassette in her lap. A stray lock of blond hair dangled in front of her bent head, and I could see the tip of her tongue sticking out of the corner of her mouth. She was intent on the task of rewinding the typewriter ribbon, looking for evidence that it had been used to type the phony ransom notes, and barely grunted an acknowledgment of my arrival.

"Any luck?"

She shook her head without looking up. "Not yet, but I'm getting close to our target dates."

"Take a break," I said. "I want both of you to see this." I took the lighter from my pocket, and laid it on the desk.

Gus picked up the lighter and turned it over in his hand, his lips pursed in a silent whistle. "Nice. A Dunhill." He looked at the bottom. "14K gold." He looked up. "Where did you come by this?"

I pointed to the monogram. "What do you make of that?"

"Looks like G.S. Where'd you get this, Dick?"

I explained where and when I had found the lighter, then repeated the story Cosmo had told during the interrogation. Millie looked up at the mention of Mr. G. "Who are you suggesting gave him the lighter?" she asked. "Gordon Sethwick?"

"The thought crossed my mind," I admitted.

Millie looked unconvinced. "I don't think he's the type."

"What do you mean?"

173

She placed the typewriter cassette on Gus's desk, stood, and leaned against the back of her chair. "Ah, that's better," she said. "My back was starting to hurt."

"About Sethwick," I prompted. "You've been working for him a couple of days now. What do you think of him?"

"He's a reasonable boss," she hedged.

"That's not what I meant, Millie."

"I don't think he murdered Celine, if that's what you're asking."

"Or paid for someone else to kill her?" Gus chimed in.

"No, not that, either. I think he was still in love with her." She nodded her head. "In fact, I'm sure of it. He visits her grave every evening. His wife has been giving him hell over it. Says that his behavior is unseemly."

"But that hasn't stopped him?"

"No, and it's really pissing her off. She's used to being obeyed."

"Even by her husband?" I asked.

"Especially by her husband. Sylvia Sutherland wears the pants in that office - at home, too, I would imagine." Millie retrieved the cassette from the desk, sat back down, and resumed rewinding the tape. I checked my watch. It was getting close to 7:00. I grabbed the lighter and replaced it in my pocket.

"I'll check in with you tomorrow, Gus." I gave Millie a peck on the back of the neck. "Keep plugging away, kid. I'm going to have another talk with Gordon Sethwick."

I retrieved my car from its parking spot behind Gus's building and headed for the cemetery. Traffic was light, and I drove through the open gates just as the digital clock on the dashboard flipped to 7:30.

I drove slowly along the one-way lane, watching for the Sutherland enclosure. I spotted Sethwick's sedan, which was parked directly in front of a snappy emerald-green BMW M1. I backed up, parked out of sight of the other vehicles, and approached on foot. As I got closer, I could make out three people standing by Celine's grave. I crouched down behind a convenient memorial stone and waited. Sylvia - it was impossible to not recognize her voice, even at a distance - was arguing with Sethwick, insisting that he come home with her and Susan, who must have just arrived in town. I didn't dare to move, even though my legs were cramping and I was worried that someone might decide to visit Mollie and Jacob Warner, who were resting in peace next to each other and approximately six feet under me. Finally, Sylvia stormed off, flinging a "Stay, then, and be damned to you!" over her shoulder as she stalked back to the Beemer. Susan hesitated long enough to pat Sethwick on the arm, then turned to join Sylvia. I waited until their car was out of sight, stood up, and walked quietly over to the Sutherland enclosure.

"Mind if I join you?"

Startled, Sethwick whirled around at the sound of my voice. "You again. What the hell are you doing here?"

"I need to talk to you."

Sethwick stalked up to me until his face was about six inches from mine. I looked at him in the gentle dusk of the July evening. His eyes were bloodshot and red-rimmed, his face deeply lined and gray with fatigue. He had aged ten years in the past 24 hours. "I have nothing more to say to you," he grated through clenched teeth. "Get lost."

"You're wrong, Sethwick." It was an effort, but I managed to keep my voice calm. "We have a lot to talk about."

"What, for instance?"

"This." I reached into my pocket, took out the lighter, and held it up for him to see. Even in the fading light, he recognized it immediately.

"Where did you get that?" he asked, his voice sinking to a husky whisper.

"Found it. Fell out of the pocket of a murder suspect," I told him, my tone harsher than before. "Now can we talk?"

He didn't reply, just heaved a sigh that ended in a shudder, the gray of his face suddenly taking on a greenish cast. He swayed on his feet, and I put out my hand to steady him.

"You OK?" I asked.

He nodded slowly in reply. "Haven't had much sleep these last days."

"I haven't eaten yet," I told him. "Is there someplace we could grab a coffee and a bite?"

He reacted sluggishly, as though he was hearing and speaking a foreign language and translating each word individually. "Yeah. There's a doughnut shop not far from here. You can follow me in your car."

I walked back to my car and tailed him to a small café sporting a flashing neon sign that read 'Duncan's Donuts. Open 24 Hours.' We pulled into the parking lot and walked inside. Sethwick headed over to a corner table and collapsed into one of the seats. I walked over to the counter, where I ordered two extra-large coffees and a six-pack of assorted doughnuts. I brought them over to the table and slid into the seat across from Sethwick. He nodded a silent acknowledgment as he lifted his styrofoam coffee cup to his lips. When he put the cup back down, his trembling hands caused some of the liquid to slosh onto the chipped Formica table top.

"I needed that," he said, a tremor in his voice.

I sipped at my coffee, bit into a jelly doughnut, and waited. The silence lengthened as we drank our coffee and demolished the doughnuts. Sethwick reached into a jacket pocket and pulled out a flip-top pack of Lucky Strikes. He tilted the top of the pack in my direction. "Smoke?"

I shook my head. "No, thanks. But you go ahead." I paused, then asked, "Run out of Sutherlands?"

His mouth twisted into a grimace. "Don't like them much."

"The Sutherlands or the smokes?"

His pupils contracted at my sally. He grunted in reply and started fishing in his pockets. "Can you give me a light?"

I said nothing as I took the Dunhill from my pocket, nonchalantly flicked it to life, and held the flame for him as he stared at the lighter. "Where did you say you got that?" he asked.

"Off a murder suspect," I repeated. "I told you that already."

"Who?" he insisted. "Where?"

"Why should I tell you?"

"Because it's my lighter!" His voice was rising, and the counter clerk glanced in our direction.

"What makes you so sure that it's yours?"

"The monogram. The 'G.S.' It's my lighter, I tell you. Give it to me."

I stood the lighter on the table beside my crumb-filled napkin. "How did you lose it?" I asked him.

"I don't know." He rubbed his eyes with the heels of his hands. "I always keep it in the inside breast pocket of my jacket. When I reached for it one day a couple of weeks ago, it was gone." He buried his face in his hands. "She gave it to me for my birthday," he said, his voice muffled.

"Who?" I asked. "Your wife?"

"No, not Sylvia." He lifted his head and looked at me through eyes swimming in unshed tears. "Celine," he whispered. "Celine gave it to me. Please." He held out his hand for the lighter. "It's all I have left of her."

Sethwick's eyes were on the lighter, but their focus was on the past. "We were in love," he said, half to himself. "I loved her. She was my good angel."

I looked at him. "I don't get it."

"Huh?" His eyes snapped back to me. "What don't you get?"

"You and Sylvia," I said. "If you felt that way about Celine, how did you end up with Sylvia?"

He shrugged impatiently. "The usual reason," he said, each word dragging itself out from between his clenched teeth. I leaned back in my chair, my eyes holding his, waiting to hear him say it. "I got her pregnant," he admitted finally. He continued, the words coming faster - spilling over each other as though a dam had burst. "I started working at Sutherland's under Sylvia in the Finance Department in '68 - she was CFO then. The Old Man had recruited me out of the MBA program at Harvard. Celine was studying at Bennington College in Vermont, but came home for the summer at the end of her freshman year. She spent the summer working in accounting, across the hall from me. We fell in love, and dated all summer.

He paused, a gentle smile relieving the lines of tension and sorrow on his face as he remembered their summer love, then took up the story once more, his face growing dark. "Celine went back to Bennington the week before Labor Day. Sylvia asked me to work with her over the holiday weekend to help her prepare for an audit. She seduced me in her office. My office, now," he added with a grimace.

"How…" I began, but he waved me silent.

"She was persistent; I was young. Flattered, I guess, that the most mature and powerful of the Sutherland sisters found me attractive. Call it hormones. Stupid, but there you are." He dropped his head into his hands and stayed that way for a couple of minutes. When he looked back up, his eyes were glistening. "Anyway," he continued, "Sylvia seemed to lose interest in me after that. Celine and I arranged to meet at an inn up in the Catskills the weekend before Thanksgiving - she was coming home for the holiday. When I returned to Atlantic City from the Catskills, Sylvia confronted me. Told me she was pregnant and the baby was mine. 'What do you want me to do?' I asked her. 'I'll do whatever you want,' I promised. 'Then marry me,' she said. 'Marry me at Christmas.'

"Sylvia announced our engagement over Thanksgiving dinner. I'll never forget the look of betrayal on Celine's face. She left for Bennington that night. That was the last I saw of her until the Old Man's funeral."

"What happened to the baby - yours and Sylvia's?" I asked.

"There wasn't one." Sethwick shook his head, a pattern of bitter lines settling around his eyes and mouth. "She claimed that she miscarried, but I think she lied. I don't think there ever was a baby. She just used me to hurt Celine."

"Why did you stay with her, then?"

"Why not?" he shrugged. "I'd lost Celine. What else did I have to lose? If I left Sylvia, I'd be leaving a promising career. And I told myself that, if I stayed, maybe somehow things would work out. Between Celine and me, I mean. I thought, maybe, there was a chance when she came back to work at Sutherland's. But she barely gave me

179

the time of day, except to discuss business. Then she got mixed up with those employees who came to her with that cock-and-bull story that I was cooking the books. I was furious at her accusations, although I guess I can understand why she believed their claims. I told her to mind her own business if she knew what was good for her."

"And now she's dead."

"Yes. Now she's dead." His face was stark, as he repeated the words. "Now she's dead. " He shook his head, his eyes straying back to the lighter.

"What do you know about a guy named Cosmo?" I asked, following his gaze.

"Who?"

"Cosmo," I repeated. "His real name is Tiberias Poindexter. He claims that a person calling himself 'Mr. G.' gave him this lighter a few days before the 'Christmas in July' ball."

Sethwick looked both puzzled and defensive. "What are you trying to say?"

"Celine's murder was premeditated - carefully planned. Cosmo was part of the attempt to set me up as the fall guy." I stood and returned the lighter to my pocket. "Be warned, Sethwick. The cops will be wanting to interview you. This lighter links you to Cosmo."

He grabbed my left wrist. "Wait, Dickens."

I reached over with my right hand and pried his hand away. "So long, Sethwick."

Traffic was light, and it took me only twenty minutes to get back to town. I detoured past Gus's office on my way home. His lights were still on, so I parked my car and went upstairs.

"Perfect timing, Dick." Gus saluted me with a raised can of Sam Adams. "We're celebrating."

I turned to Millie, who was looking inordinately pleased with herself.

"You found it?"

"I sure did." Her brief nod belied the triumphant gleam in her eyes. "I had to rewind the ribbon almost to the start of this puppy," she said, waving the typewriter cartridge in the air. "But it was worth it. I found every single one of those fake notes - including the one that Sylvia Sutherland used to convince you to go to the Steel Pier the night of Celine's murder."

"Can you tell when the notes were typed?"

"To the day. Dated letters were typed that same day using the same ribbon cartridge, bracketing the fake ransom notes. My guess is that whoever used the machine to produce the ransom notes did so during lunch hour, while the front office was deserted."

"Millie, you're a miracle worker!" I leaned down and gave her a hug that threatened to overturn her beer.

"Careful, Dick," she giggled, holding the can in the air. "You're jostling Sam.

Gus handed me a can. "Here," he said. "Join the party."

I shook my head and waved it off. "Thanks, Gus, but I'm bushed. I just spent some time with Sethwick."

"Oh?" they chorused.

"Tell you about it tomorrow." I turned to Millie. "Why don't you give me that IBM cartridge?" I suggested. "I'll turn it in to Lt. Holmes tomorrow morning, and walk him through its significance. I have to return the cigarette lighter to him, anyway."

Millie handed the cartridge to Gus, who placed it in a large brown envelope, which he sealed. Carefully, he wrote

181

July 31, 1979 across the flap, signed his name, then pushed the envelope across his desk. "Here, Millie," he explained. "Sign your name across the flap under my signature. That way, Holmes can testify that he received a sealed envelope, and we can testify as to its contents before it left our possession."

"Good call," I commented, taking the envelope from Millie. "I'll try to catch Holmes when he gets into his office." I headed for the door. "Enjoy your celebration," I said as I turned and waved good-bye. "I'm going home to bed."

Twenty-eight

I arrived at police headquarters just before eight-thirty the next morning. But I might just as well have stayed in bed for all the good it did me. A uniformed officer named Klauptmann - an officious oaf if ever I met one - took obvious delight in informing me at fifteen-minute intervals that Lt. Holmes was engaged. Finally, at five to ten, I was escorted upstairs. "Thanks for seeing me," I began as I walked through the door to Holmes's office. He looked up, scowling. "Oh, it's you."

"Have I done something?" I asked.

"No, no... grab a seat, Dickens." He waved me over to the chair in front of his desk. "Sorry. It's been a lousy morning."

I sat and opened my briefcase. "Here," I said, leaning forward to hand him the typewriter cartridge, still sealed in its bulky brown envelope. "This might help."

He turned the envelope over, feeling its bulk, and eyeing the dated signatures on the sealed flap. "What's all this?"

I explained to him how Millie had identified the location of the typewriter on which the Sutherland ransom notes - the notes intended to frame me - were typed. He nodded as he listened, but seemed distracted, as he turned the envelope over and over in his hands. "Is that all?" he asked.

"Not quite." Reaching into my pocket, I retrieved the cigarette lighter and placed it on his desk. "I was able to confirm that this lighter belongs to Gordon Sethwick. He claims that he lost it a couple of weeks ago," I added.

Holmes reached forward and pushed the lighter back towards me. "You may as well give this back to him," he growled. "Can't use it."

"Why not?" I was looking directly at him, but his eyes refused to meet mine. So I sat and let the silence grow thick. At last, he placed both hands palm down on his desk top, half-rose from his chair, and landed his bombshell.

"We had to let Cosmo go this morning," he said, sitting back down with a thud.

I opened my mouth to protest, but he held up a hand to stop me. "Hear me out, Dickens." His voice was harsh as he forced the words past his lips. "The D.A. decided that he couldn't make the conspiracy charge stick on the say-so of a single witness. No corroborating evidence, he claims. So we had to let Cosmo go."

"But, what about Benny Caravaggio's murder?" I protested. "What happened to the eyewitness at that propane company in Everettville? Didn't he come down to ID Cosmo?"

"Yeah. First thing this morning."

"So?"

"So all Cosmo did was ask this witness for directions. That's not a crime in this state, last I checked."

"But…"

"But what?" Holmes snapped. "We have no eyewitness to the crime. We have no physical evidence placing Cosmo - or anyone else - at the scene. And we haven't found the murder weapon. What the hell do you expect me to do? Wave a magic wand?" He drew a deep breath, let it out slowly, and continued in a more conversational tone. "Look, Dickens. I've been dealing with this ever since I got in this morning. There was a little twerp of a newly minted attorney lying in wait for me in the parking lot, spouting *habeas corpus* as though he had invented the concept. I. Had. No. Choice."

I held up my right hand, palm forward. "Wait. Back up a second. You mean to tell me that you never found the murder weapon?"

"No sign of it in the cabin where the victim was shot, or in the woods around the cabin. No sign of it in Cosmo's house, or in the garage where he keeps his bike. Not stashed on the bike or at the biker's clubhouse, either. We looked. Nada."

"What about the septic tank?"

"The wha.....?"

"Benny's body was shoved into a septic tank. Remember? Did the Everettville sheriff's crime scene investigation team dredge the tank?"

Holmes's eyes widened in understanding. "Good question, Dickens. I never thought to ask. I'll check on that right away." He allowed himself a flicker of a smile. "Now get out of here. I don't have time to sit and jaw with you. I have work to do."

I left - but not before I wrung a promise from Holmes to maintain police protection on Bruno and Sophia Caravaggio. I was feeling prickles at the back of my neck as I walked back to my car. Events were moving toward some sort of climax. I just didn't know what or where. I decided to head for my office and try to reason things through.

I unlocked the door and found the usual avalanche of flyers and bills that had been shoved through the mail slot. I picked them up automatically and headed for my desk, leafing through the stack as I walked. I had just sat down and was starting to separate the bills from the rest of the junk when I was interrupted by the phone.

"Dickens," I announced as I lifted the receiver to my ear.

"Oh, Dick!" It was Millie - breathing hard and sounding worried. "Thank God you're there. I've been trying and trying to reach you."

"I was tied up with Holmes," I said by way of explanation. "What's up?"

"It's Susan."

"What about Susan?"

"She's disappeared!"

I sat up straight and gripped the receiver with white knuckles. "Start from the beginning, Millie," I instructed. "Tell me everything that happened."

"Well," she began, "you remember that she was supposed to meet here today with the family attorney? Arnold Barnstable?"

"Yeah, I remember. She drove down from Vermont yesterday. I caught a glimpse of her yesterday evening at the cemetery."

"Well, she came in this morning with Sylvia and Sethwick," Millie continued, her words spilling over each other. "They all went into the conference room - the three of them and Mr. Barnstable, the attorney. About eight-thirty or so. Then Sethwick came out, muttering something about a 'fool's errand,' and left without a word about how long he'd be gone." She stopped.

"Millie, are you still there?"

"Oh, sorry, Dick. I thought I heard a noise. I'm all alone here."

"What happened next?" I did a quick mental double-take. "What do you mean you're all alone? Where is everyone?"

"Today's the company picnic, Dick. We only have a skeleton staff on hand in the building. I'm just a temp, so I was volunteered to miss the picnic and handle the executive front office for the day."

"Okay. Got it. What happened after Sethwick stormed out?"

"Sylvia came out of the conference room about 10 minutes after Sethwick left. She was agitated. She told me that Susan had complained of being dizzy and nauseated, then vomited and passed out. Sylvia tossed me her car keys and told me to bring the car around to the back of the building - the executive office has an exit directly to the rear parking area. She and Mr. Barnstable would help Susan downstairs, and they were going to take her to the ER. She explained that it would be quicker than waiting for an ambulance."

"Haven't you heard anything since they left?"

"That's just it, Dick," Millie explained. "They left here around 9 o'clock and I went back upstairs to watch the phones and to wait for Sethwick to return. He got back around 9:30. I told him what happened, and he raced back out. I called the hospital shortly after he left. I wanted to know how Susan was. But the ER had no record of her. I thought there might be a mixup - you know, the name misspelled or something. But they said it had been a quiet morning. Not a single emergency."

"Maybe she was feeling better, and Sylvia decided to take her to the house, instead?" I ventured.

"I thought of that, Dick. I called the house. There was no answer. Not even a machine picked up." Millie stopped and caught her breath. "Dick, I'm worried."

I thought for a moment. "Can you find out the name of Sylvia's doctor? Maybe she took Susan to her doctor's office instead of to the ER."

"Maybe. She keeps a Rolodex on her desk. Hang on while I ..... NO!!!!! Dickie, help me.........." There was a muffled grunt; the receiver clattered against something solid as it fell from Millie's hand. Then I heard a click, and the line went dead.

Twenty-nine

Millie was in danger! And it was all my fault. I should never have allowed her to go back to the Sutherland offices. I flew downstairs to my car, and left about 5000 miles worth of tire rubber behind as I took off for the Sutherland complex. Pedal to the metal and hand on the horn, I wove in and out of traffic, kicking and cursing myself at every red light. And, I swear, I must have hit every single red light. An eternity later, I drove up to the Sutherland admin building, sprang out of the car, and ran inside. I sped past the reception desk and took the stairs up to the second floor without breaking stride. I sprinted down the hall and burst through the door to the executive offices.

The front office area was deserted. Millie's desk was painfully tidy - as though she had never used it. There was no sign of a struggle. But a faint whiff of Chanel No. 5 in the air was all I needed to confirm that she had been there that day. There was something else, though. I sniffed the air again, trying to separate the scents. And then I recognized it. A trace of a familiar odor. Chloroform. Some bastard had chloroformed Millie!

I heard a voice coming from Sethwick's office. I opened his door just as he hung up the phone. He looked up at me, his eyes registering confusion, anger, and just a hint of fear. "Everyone's gone," he said, his forehead wrinkled in puzzlement. "Susan, Sylvia, everyone."

"Gone where?" I asked him. He didn't reply - just stared at me. I reached across his desk and shook him by the shoulders. "Come on, man. Where have they gone?"

He held up a folded piece of note paper. "Vermont," he replied. "They've gone to Vermont." He unfolded and folded the piece of paper in his hands over and over as he continued.

"I found this note from Sylvia on my front door. It says, 'Susan needs a rest. I'm taking her to the lodge.' "

"The lodge?"

"That's the family ski house in Stowe," he explained.

"What happened this morning, Sethwick? Did Susan look ill to you?"

"She seemed fine," he said. "We had a meeting scheduled with Barney. To talk about Celine's will."

"Barney?"

"Sorry," Sethwick shook his head rapidly back and forth, trying to clear his thoughts. "Arnold Barnstable. He prefers Barney."

"Barnstable," I interjected. "Isn't he one of the executives here?"

"He's the Corporate Secretary. Handles the legal stuff - board meeting minutes, corporate filings. Stuff like that. But he's also been the Sutherland family's attorney since before I signed on."

I nodded. "Go on. So the meeting was to talk about Celine's will."

"Her wills, actually."

"There was more than one?"

"Two wills. Apparently, Celine made a will naming her son as her sole heir," he explained, "with Sylvia and Barney as co-executors and co-trustees. That was several years ago, shortly after the Old Man died." He looked up at me, then back down at his hands for what felt like an eternity before he began again, bitterness and despair mingling in his voice. "Her son. I never knew that Celine had a child. Sylvia's known about him for a long time, but she never told me until after Celine was killed," he added. "The other day, Susan called Sylvia and said she needed to discuss Celine's new will. It names Susan as sole trustee

190

for Celine's estate and as her executor. Some attorney in Vermont drew it up just a couple of weeks ago."

I sat quietly. Even though I was frantic to start looking for Millie, I didn't want to interrupt his flood of words.

"We convened here this morning in the conference room," he went on. "We had just helped ourselves to coffee when Sylvia suddenly 'remembered' a message she needed to convey to Mary Sue Thorpe, our head of Human Resources. Mary Sue was in charge of the company picnic. Sylvia insisted that I head right over to the Egg Harbor Country Club and give Mary Sue the message. So I left. I didn't get back until about nine-thirty. Millie told me that Susan had fallen ill. When she reported that Sylvia and Barney had taken Susan to the ER, I drove over to the hospital to see how she was."

He stopped and shook his head, clearly still unsure what had happened. "But they never arrived. I called the house from the ER. There was no answer, so I drove home and found this note on the door. I came back here, and the place was empty. Even Millie was gone. I tried calling Barney's law office just now, but his secretary said that he wasn't expected in today. There's no answer at his apartment, either. Everybody's gone." He shook his head, his voice plaintive and trailing off. "They're all gone," he repeated, then looked up at me, a glazed look in his eyes. "What are you doing here?"

"Millie called me," I said shortly. "To tell me about Susan. Someone attacked Millie while she was talking to me on the phone. I heard it happen. I don't know who has taken her or why, but I aim to find out." I locked my eyes on his. "I don't think Susan's sudden illness was an accident. I suspect she was poisoned. And I know that Millie was chloroformed. I smelled the chloroform in your outer office as soon as I walked in. Will you help me find them?" He said nothing - just stared at me with empty eyes. I strode around to where he sat, grabbed him by the necktie, and slapped both his cheeks with the flat of my hand. "Snap out of it, man" I shouted. "There are three lives at stake."

"Three?" He looked at me, still dazed, his cheeks bright red where I had slapped him. "Who?"

"Three," I repeated. "Susan, Millie, and Arthur, Jr. - Celine's son." I hesitated, silently asking Celine's forgiveness if I was making the wrong choice, then added. "Your son."

"My son?" His eyes widened as he realized what I had just revealed. He squared his shoulders, pressed his hands to the top of his desk, and straightened his posture. "My son?" he repeated. "Where is he?"

"With his foster parents," I answered. "In Vermont. They live in Stowe, Vermont."

Sethwick rose abruptly from his desk. "What are we waiting for?" he demanded. "Let's go!"

I looked at his 6'2" frame. "We'd better take your car," I suggested. "You won't fit in mine."

"Who said anything about driving?"

"Huh?"

"I keep a Cessna 180 at Bader Field," he explained. "It'll get us there in half the time."

"What about a pilot?"

"You're looking at him." Sethwick smiled fleetingly. "I learned how to fly in the Air Force ROTC. After I married Sylvia, I bought my first plane and I started to fly regularly for relaxation. Up there, I'm the one in control."

"Uh, how big is this plane?"

"Oh, plenty big enough. It's a four-seater. Let's go, Dickens," he urged. "Time's a-wasting."

"We need to get one thing straight first, Sethwick."

"What's that?"

"My friends call me Dick. " I held out my right hand and he grasped it firmly in his.

"Call me Seth," he said.

"Not 'Gordon'?"

"Only one person ever called me 'Gordon.' " He squeezed his eyes shut, and I could see him convulse briefly as he struggled to control his emotions. "But she's dead." He bent his head for a moment, then lifted his chin, determination transforming his face and posture "Let's go, Dick. I need to prepare and file a flight plan before we take off."

"You're the pilot," I said. "I have to make one stop. Let's take both cars, and meet at Bader Field."

I drove back to the city and burst into Gus's office unannounced. "Gus, I need that package you've been holding for me. Also, I need a gun. The cops still have mine."

"What's going on, Dick?" he asked. "You look like you've been wrestling with ghosts."

"Susan and Millie have been kidnapped," I replied, filling him in quickly on the morning's events. "Sethwick and I are going after them. I need you to call Holmes, and have him send a crime scene team to the Sutherland offices before the conference room gets cleaned up. Tell him that one of the coffee cups may have been spiked with something - a toxin or drug that causes nausea and vomiting."

Gus's eyes widened when I told him that Sethwick and I were going to fly up to Vermont on a rescue mission in Sethwick's Cessna, but he made no comment - just walked over to his safe and spun the dial of the combination lock. He reached in and extracted a Smith & Wesson .32 snub-nose revolver, a box of cartridges, and the envelope I had sent to him for safekeeping, and handed them over to me. He closed the safe and spun the dial to reset the lock. "I'll take care of things at this end," he assured me. "You can count on me."

"I always do. Thanks Gus," I added as I turned to go. "Thanks for everything."

I unlocked my car, tossed the envelope on the front passenger seat, and slid behind the wheel. I took Tennessee to Atlantic, then hung a right. Bader Field was just a couple of miles away, and I covered the distance in less than 10 minutes. I pulled into the parking lot, grabbed the envelope, and extracted a small, lumpy pouch and a slip of paper with an address written on it, tucking them both into the inner pocket of my jacket. I loaded the .32, verified that the trigger lock was engaged, and slipped the gun into my trouser pocket. My briefcase was in the trunk. I transferred the envelope into the case and slammed the trunk lid shut. Then I locked the car and set off in search of the General Aviation terminal.

Bader Field was Atlantic City's first municipal airport. But it had been unable to compete with the newer - though less convenient - Atlantic City International Airport. One by one, the major airlines defected. Now, Bader was the domain of puddle jumpers and private pilots. I spotted a large "General Aviation" sign above a set of glass doors; Sethwick was standing at a counter just inside. I walked up and announced that I was 'all set,' in spite of a colony of butterflies that had taken up residence in the pit of my stomach. "Perfect timing, Dick," he responded. "I was just checking the weather. It rained up there yesterday, but we'll have clear skies today. Let's go."

I followed him out to the apron. He wove confidently between the rows of parked Cessnas, Pipers, and other pipsqueaks that looked like oversized boy's toys. Stopping suddenly, he slapped the side of one of the planes. "Here she is," he said. "The door's unlocked. Hop on board and get comfortable while I complete my pre-flight check. There's a headset on the seat. Put it on and plug the cable into the instrument panel."

I clambered into the front passenger seat and noticed to my consternation that it was equipped with a set of controls and instruments. Was I expected to help fly this thing? I craned my neck to see what Sethwick was up to. He was poking and prodding the wings, moving bits and pieces around. He climbed onto the wing, which was centered over the top of the passenger cabin - didn't even look like a real airplane, I muttered to myself; the wings were in the wrong place - unscrewed a cap, and dipped what appeared to be a turkey baster into what he later identified as the gas tank. Need to make sure there's no water in the fuel, he explained. I decided not to ask what would have happened if he had found any.

Finally, he climbed into his seat, donned his head set, fastened his seat belt, and gave me an abbreviated safety briefing. When he saw that I was securely belted in, he yelled, "Clear Prop!" and started the engine. The propeller stammered and sputtered briefly, then caught. He taxied to the runway, stopped, and spoke some mumbo-jumbo into his microphone. The control tower must have liked what he had to say, because the next thing I knew, we were rolling.

Thirty

I shut my eyes and gripped my knees tightly with my hands - there were no armrests to grab - as we gathered speed. Something was chattering in synchrony with the vibration of the plane. I knew it couldn't be my teeth, because my jaws were clamped as tightly shut as my eyes. Then there was a slight thunk and the vibration ceased. I felt everything tilt to the left. Oh no, no, no, I thought, we're going to crash.

"You can open your eyes, Dick." I could hear the amusement in Seth's voice. "We're on our way."

I squinted one eye open. We were in a climbing turn. All I could see out my window was blue sky and a few puffy clouds. I turned my head and looked out the left side of the plane. "Hey, we're over water. What are we doing over water?"

"Relax, Dick. I know what I'm doing." He handed me a map and pointed to a thick red zig-zag line oriented roughly north-south. There were some numbers written next to the line wherever it changed directions. "This is our flight plan," he explained. "We're over water because I want to avoid all the air traffic around New York - especially JFK and La Guardia. We'll cut over the middle of Long Island, and aim for New Haven. We're flying VFR; that's 'visual flight rules.' You can assistant-navigate for me. Watch for the landmarks that show on this map - rivers, highways, railway tracks - and let me know when you see them. When we hit New Haven, I want to pick up Interstate 91. We'll let it lead us to the Connecticut River, then follow the river upstream as far as White River Junction. From there, we head along the Interstate 89 to Waterbury, Vermont, latch onto Route 100 and follow it straight to the Morrisville-Stowe airport. Piece of pie."

"Don't you mean piece of cake?"

"Nah. I'm a pie kinda guy." This was a totally different Sethwick. Relaxed, self-assured. In control. I could feel some of the tension bleeding out of my body.

"What do we do for transportation when we land?" I wondered. "Is there a car rental place at this airport?"

"No need. I keep a car garaged nearby. I've already called ahead and told them to have it gassed up and waiting for us."

We fell silent for a while, but it was a comfortable quiet. We had just crossed the south shore of Long Island, and I could see the Sound on the horizon when Sethwick broke the silence. "I took Celine up a couple of times in a rented plane the summer we were dating," he reminisced. "We would just fly around off-shore and enjoy having 'slipped the surly bonds of earth.' " I must have looked puzzled, because he added. "From my favorite poem. 'High Flight.' Written by a World War II flyer named John Gillespie Magee, Jr. The last line of the poem goes '...put out my hand and touched the face of God.' " He nodded and swallowed a couple of times before continuing, his voice gentle. "That's how it felt, with Celine. Like touching the face of God."

He paused, then spoke again, his words now ringing like tempered steel. "I failed Celine," he said. "I'm not going to fail our son. Or Susan." He reached out his right hand and gave my left shoulder a brief squeeze. "Or your Millie," he added.

"You focus on the boy, Seth," I told him. "I'll take care of Susan and Millie."

"But..."

"Listen to me," I said. "There are only two people who know where he is."

"Where 'he' is," Sethwick echoed. "You mean Arthur."

"Yeah, I mean Arthur. Arthur G. Sutherland." I saw his mouth open and anticipated his next question. "And, yes, the 'G' stands for Gordon. Now, listen, Seth." I began again. "The only people who know where Arthur lives - and with whom - are Susan and me." I stopped and considered. "Well, maybe also the Vermont lawyer who drew up Celine's new will. But that's it. No one else knows. Yet."

"You mean..."

"That's right. They'll probably try to force Susan to lead them to Arthur. And they won't be squeamish about it, either. We have a time window, and we need to use it."

Seth nodded. "I think I see where you're going. You want me to move Arthur and his foster parents to safety while you go after Susan and Millie."

"That's it."

"There's a police station in Morrisville," Seth thought out loud. "I could take them there, then join up with you at the lodge."

"Sounds like a plan," I agreed. "Be sure to bring a posse with you."

"Count on it." He held out his right hand, and I gripped it in mine.

"I do," I replied. "Partner."

After that, there wasn't much left to say. The plane droned on, Connecticut scenery giving way to Massachusetts scenery and then to Vermont greenery, as first the Connecticut River then the White River glittered below us in the afternoon sun. From where I was sitting, all three states looked pretty much alike, except that the towns grew smaller and sparser, and the vegetation greener and more dense, the farther north we flew. I was sunk in a brown study. Would we be too late? I had failed to protect Celine. Had I blown it again? Were Susan and Millie already dead?

The plane banked to the right, and I looked over at Seth. "You were about 7,500 feet away," he said.

"A million miles, you mean."

"No. I meant 7,500 feet. Our altitude at the moment."

"I don't get you." I wondered whether the air was thin enough up here that it had affected his reason.

"I meant that you looked as though you wanted to be on the ground and under your own steam," he explained. "It won't be long now. That's Route 100 below us. We're only about ten miles from the airport." He tilted his head to the left, using it as a pointer. "Over that way is Mt. Mansfield. There's a narrow road that crests the ridge at Smuggler's Notch. Named for the whiskey runners who used it to smuggle contraband from Canada during prohibition. Treacherous road at night or in bad weather. It's just one lane at the top, with a sharp curve around some large boulders. Great ski runs on both sides of the mountain in winter, though."

"What's that other peak out there?" I wondered, pointing to the right out my side window.

"Oh, that's the Stowe Pinnacle. Decent hiking trails. There's a view of it from the lodge." Seth tensed slightly, and started fiddling with some of the controls. I noticed a slight change in the sound and vibration of the engine. "There it is," Seth pointed. "At about one o'clock. That's the airport."

I peered out the windshield in the indicated direction. "That little thing?" I asked. "It looks no bigger than a country lane. Are you sure you haven't taken a wrong turn?"

"It gets bigger as we get closer. We're still a few miles out." He reached over and tugged at my seat belt, making sure it was secure. "Okay," he said. "Here we go."

Seth spoke a few words to someone about making a straight-in approach, and acknowledged the reply. He pulled some levers, pressed a button or two and, in a shorter time than I expected, the runway looked much larger than before. I had a fleeting impression that the ground was rising to meet us. Then there was a brief thump, and we were rolling along on the tarmac. He taxied the plane off the runway, eased into what he told me was his usual parking space, and switched off the engine.

We clambered out of the cabin just as a fellow in coveralls trotted up to greet us. Seth talked to him for a couple of minutes while the guy put chocks under the wheels to keep the plane from rolling, then anchored it to the ground with a set of cables. I stood by impatiently, shifting my weight from left foot to right and back again, waiting for them to finish.

"That's my mechanic," Seth explained as we headed for a one-story building that proudly proclaimed this to be the Morrisville-Stowe Airport. "I told him to check out the plane and gas her up - in case we need to make a quick getaway." He slowed, and pointed to a desk. "I need to report in," he added. "Then we can go."

While Seth took care of his business, I searched out the men's room to take care of some business of my own. I used the privacy to double-check that my revolver was loaded and ready. After confirming that the trigger lock was still engaged, I returned the gun to my pocket and went to meet Seth. I followed him through a door marked EXIT over to a freshly washed sky-blue Subaru wagon parked at the curb. "This is it," he said, pulling a key ring from his pocket. "Hop in."

"This is your car?"

"Yeah. Nothing like a Subaru for Vermont winter driving," he added. "All-wheel drive, you know." We got into the car, and he started the engine. "I told my dealer they should promote the Subaru as the unofficial state car of Vermont. Told him I'd expect a commission if the ad campaign worked." He smiled briefly, inviting a reply, but I couldn't think of a snappy comeback. I shrugged instead. "Let's see what this baby will do," I said.

"Where are we going?"

I pulled the slip of paper out of my jacket pocket and read the address to him "526 Worcester Loop," I told him.

He looked puzzled. "Spell it," he asked.

"W-O-R-C-E-S-T-E-R."

"Oh," he nodded. "You mean 'Wooster' Loop. "I know where that is. Just off Mansfield View, between here and the center of town."

We turned left out of the parking lot onto Route 100. I rolled down my window, then quickly rolled it back up. "What is that stink?" I asked, stunned by the cloying, earthy sweetness that had set up housekeeping in my nostrils.

"Manure," Seth replied. "Most popular fertilizer around here - dairy farmers share it with their neighbors."

We passed a garden center on our left, after which a series of corn fields bracketed both sides of the road. By the time I had expelled the lingering remnants of manure from my lungs, Seth was activating his left turn signal. "Mansfield View," he announced. "We're almost there."

His navigation was spot on. Two more turns about a quarter-mile apart, and we were on Worcester Loop. I spotted a mail box with "526" on it; Seth made a final right turn into the short lane next to the mail box and shut off the engine. Facing us was a small A-frame house, set on about one acre of cleared land. The exterior was clapboard, painted pine-needle green; the window frames, fascias, and eaves were the color of semi-sweet chocolate. Brown asphalt shingles flecked with green covered the steep-pitched roof. Pine decking wrapped itself around two sides of the structure, a few inches off the ground. There was a separate small shed located towards the rear of the clearing, and a Ford pick-up truck parked beside the house. A couple of white-tail deer looked up from their grazing when we opened the car doors, and then sauntered off in search of a more private location for their afternoon snack. I mounted the two stone steps that led to the door, with Seth a couple of paces behind me.

Thirty-one

Someone must have heard the car, because the door opened a crack before I had a chance to knock. "Yes?" The voice was female; the tone wary.

"Mrs. Hegarty?" I began.

"Who wants to know?"

"My name is Damien Dickens." I slid my business card through the crack in the door. "I'm here on behalf of Celine."

The crack widened slightly, though I still couldn't see into the house. "Prove it," the voice commanded.

I reached into my jacket for the pouch that Celine had given me and maneuvered it through the slender opening. "Here," I said.

The door closed; Seth and I stood outside and waited, each second passing more slowly than its predecessor. Finally, I heard a security chain rattle, and the door opened to reveal a pleasantly plump woman. Mary Hegarty was about five-two or five-three. Her short, curly gray hair framed a round face that held a pair of teal blue eyes and a generous mouth. There were fan-shaped laugh lines in the corners of her eyes and mouth; a pair of Mother Goose spectacles balanced at the tip of a dainty nose. A Labrador retriever whose coat was the color of a milk chocolate Hershey bar stood at her left side, watching me alertly. Mary held the empty pouch in her left hand. A platinum earring shaped like a miniature oyster half-shell lay in the palm of her right hand. On the shell sat a perfect emerald-green pearl.

"How do I know this isn't a fake?" she asked, still leery.

"The initials 'C.S.' are etched into the back of the earring," I replied. "And Celine gave you the matching earring during her last visit. Besides," I added, "if you had any doubts as to its authenticity, you shouldn't have opened the door."

She nodded again, and her expression lost a little of its distrust. "Come in," she said, stepping away from the door. I walked through the open doorway; Mary's eyes narrowed and her expression froze when she saw who was behind me. "What is he doing here?" Her voice was cold and sharp - each word a stalactite.

"This is..."

"I know who this is," she interrupted, biting off each word. "I want to know why Gordon Sethwick is here with you."

Seth stepped past me and held Mary's gaze. "I'm here to help," he said. "I know what you think of me, Mrs. Hegarty, and I deserve it. But things have changed. I've changed."

Mary returned his gaze, probing him with her eyes. When she found what she was looking for, she nodded and ushered us inside. The interior of the house was a study in wood. Douglas fir posts supported beams and trusses of the same species. The ceilings and walls were finished in knotty pine, while clear pine planks covered the floor. The kitchen was open to view, and fit the country motif - a '50s-style oversized gas range, an enamel sink the size of a small bathtub, and knotty pine cabinetry. The countertop was a highly polished slab of Vermont granite. Mary noticed the direction of my gaze. "Zeb's a carpenter," she said, allowing her pride to show. "He built this place."

"Is he here?" I asked. "We need to talk to you both. It's urgent."

"I'll send for him." She took a pencil and paper from a kitchen drawer, scribbled a note, and attached it to the dog's collar. "Portia, go find Zeb," she ordered. "Bring him here."

With a single 'woof,' the dog squirmed through a flap in the front door and bounded off. "Zeb's in the work shed," Mary explained. "Portia knows what to do."

She led the way into the living room and invited us to sit. We obeyed, even though I begrudged every minute lost. "Where's Arthur?" I asked.

"Artie's upstairs in the loft." Mary pointed at a spiral staircase. He's doing his school work." Anticipating my next question, she added, "he's home-schooled. We thought it would be best. The Sutherland's are too well known in Stowe."

"Why settle here, then?" Seth interjected. "Why not some place more discrete?"

"We used to live in Shaftsbury, just north of Bennington," Mary explained. "But when Celine came back east and got her life back together, she asked us to move to this area so that she could visit Artie without arousing suspicions. It was natural for her to spend an occasional weekend at the family ski lodge in Stowe; it would have looked strange for her to go to Shaftsbury." Mary noticed me fidgeting - I got the feeling that she noticed most things - and turned to me. "Zeb should be here any second now."

As I was about to reply, I heard another 'woof,' and the door opened to reveal a wiry man with wavy gray hair, a furrowed face, and a grizzled beard that was neatly trimmed. He was about 5'10", and wore blue denim overalls over a white T-shirt. "I told Portia to stand watch outside," Zeb said as he walked into the house. "What's wrong? Who are these people?"

Seth and I stood, and I handled the introductions. Tersely, I explained why we had come and what needed to happen. "Seth will make sure that the three of you get to safety," I added.

"You mean four," Mary corrected. "Portia comes with us."

"Of course," I assured her. "No problem."

Seth turned to me. "You can go ahead, Dick." He handed me the car keys and a folded tourist map. "I've jotted down the directions to the lodge on this. Sylvia knows my car. When you get there, park well out of sight."

I nodded, taking the keys and map in my left hand, and clapped him on the shoulder with my right. "Good luck," I said.

"You too." He returned the gesture. "Don't worry about us. I'll see you soon."

I took my leave of Mary and Zeb. As I walked out the door, I could hear Mary's calm voice calling, "Artie, come downstairs. There's someone here I want you to meet."

After backing out of the lane, I drove down the hill and turned left onto Route 100. I was watching for a white church on the right, just past the hardware store. Following Seth's scribbled directions, I took a left turn onto School Street directly across from the church. I followed the road up the hill for just over a mile, taking care to steer left at the fork. "Look for a gravel lane on your right," Seth had explained. "There's a sign, but it's easy to miss. If you hit Cross Road, you've gone too far."

When I hit Cross Road, I turned around and retraced my track at a crawl. The signpost for Lois Lane was half-hidden by a newly planted realtor's ad that read 'Land 4 Sale. 4.7 Acres. Call Saul. 802-555-3345.' I turned into the lane, slithering through the muddy remnants of a puddle from the previous day's rain as I did so, and saw a duplicate 'For Sale' sign attached to a fence post at the entry to a driveway on my right. I turned right and followed the driveway to a tumbled down shell of a barn, pulled around the far side of the structure, and parked.

My plan was to approach the lodge on foot. I left the car unlocked and headed for the trees along the south edge of the driveway, looking back over my shoulder a couple of times to reassure myself that the Subaru was completely hidden from view. There was a slight clearing - a path of sorts - overgrown, but still navigable. I moved slowly, my ears alert for any sounds. But all I heard were cheeps and chatters. Suddenly, there was a rat-a-tat from behind. I whirled in the direction of the sound, instinctively reaching into my pocket for my gun as I dropped into a crouch. I waited, motionless, letting my eyes search from left to right and back again for the source of the noise. Nothing. I heard the rat-a-tat a second time. It seemed to be coming from above. I looked up and spotted him on my second pass - a woodpecker enjoying a bug buffet, daintily selecting his entrée from within the rotting timbers of the ramshackle old barn.

Relieved but still shaken, I returned the revolver to my pocket and resumed my cautious approach. The front of the house was visible now through the trees. To the south, the Stowe Pinnacle played peek-a-boo between the tips of the pines and the blue spruce. The lodge was constructed of ten-inch red cedar logs interlaced in a Swedish cope pattern. As Seth had described, it was accessed via a circular driveway, which passed beneath a porte-cochère that extended beyond the front portico. An attached oversized two-car garage was located at the east end of the structure. Dormers popped out from the steeply pitched shingled roof at regular intervals along the entire north face, revealing the presence of a second story. The foundation and chimney were faced in fieldstone. As far as I could tell, the place was deserted. At least, there were no cars in the driveway, and no sign of movement at any of the windows on the main level. I decided to chance a closer look.

I crept between the trees to the edge of the driveway near the west side of the house. From this vantage point, I could see that the structure was set into the side of a three-acre sloped clearing. Windows looked out over the cleared field from the first and second story, as well as from a basement level. I continued around to the back of the house. There was a full walk-out basement, with two sets of generous sliding glass doors in addition to a pair of large windows on either side of the chimney base. A broad redwood deck, bordered by a cedar log balustrade, ran along the entire south side of the main level. I could see the shimmer of late afternoon sunlight on a pond, just visible in the gaps between the trees, blueberry bushes, and blackberry canes that bordered the south edge of the clearing. I shuddered when I spotted a slight rise that signaled the presence of a septic tank near the back of the clearing. The only other structure in sight was a sort of tool shed near the bottom of the clearing to the west of the house.

I kept to the trees as long as I could, then sprinted across the cleared space to the south face of the house. Cautiously, I peered through the first set of basement doors. There was no sign of life. With my heart thumping in my throat, I tip-toed up the stairs to the deck and crept on hands and knees to the nearest window. I peeked over the window sill into what looked to be a master bedroom suite. As far as I could tell, there was no one in the room. I continued crawling along the deck to the next room - the living room - and peered through the western set of double French doors. The sofa and chairs were covered with white dust sheets. The blinking light of an activated burglar alarm system was clearly visible beyond the living room in the entrance foyer. I finished my survey at the east end of the deck; I could see the kitchen and dining room through yet another set of sliding doors. An undisturbed layer of dust the texture of powdered sugar coated the dining room table and the granite counter tops in the kitchen.

Satisfied that the house appeared unoccupied, I stood and ran the length of the deck and back down the stairs, then walked under the deck around to the east side of the structure. By squeezing between the hydrangea bushes planted along the garage wall, I was able to reach a window and look inside. I saw skis and snowshoes leaning against the far wall, but no cars. I was in luck. I had arrived in time.

Just as I finished congratulating myself, the sound of tires on gravel caught my attention. I crossed the flagstone path that paralleled the east side of the garage and crouched behind a convenient six-foot tall stack of firewood. Gaps between the stacked logs gave me peephole views of the driveway. I didn't have long to wait. In less than a minute, a cherry red Subaru station wagon with Vermont plates rolled into view and came to a stop in front of the garage. I watched Sylvia get out of the car and open the rear gate of the wagon. Slowly, painfully, two people, their hands duct-taped behind their backs, crawled backwards out of the vehicle. Sylvia grabbed each of them roughly by the arm, stood them upright, and turned them around to face her. I choked down a cry of rage mingled with relief when I saw Millie and Susan, bruised, bedraggled, and gagged with duct tape, but clearly alive and able to stand on their own.

And then my blood ran cold as I felt a gun barrel press against the skin at the base of my skull and I heard a voice say "Don't move."

Thirty-two

"Hands on your head, Dickens," the voice said. "And straighten up slowly."

I complied. "Don't turn around." The voice was familiar, but I couldn't quite place it. "Spread your legs." I glanced down and watched as a man's mirror-polished black shoe kicked my ankles farther apart. "That's it. Now don't move."

I felt him pat down my left side with his left hand. Then he switched the gun to his left hand in order to pat down my right side. "What have we here?" He gave a kind of silent whistle - a whoosh of air, really - when his hand encountered the revolver in my right trouser pocket. "I'll take care of this." I felt him shift his gun back into his right hand. The barrel had never left its place at the nape of my neck.

"Are you alright, Barney?" Sylvia called out. Barney, I nodded to myself. Arnold Barnstable. It was all starting to come together.

"Right as rain," he replied. "I've bagged me a trespasser."

I felt an extra jab of pressure from the gun barrel. "OK, Sport." He grabbed my right arm with his left hand and gave me a little yank. "Right turn. Forward march. Let's get out from behind this pile of wood. You first." He released his grip on my arm. We walked just beyond the north end of the wood pile. "That's far enough," he instructed, stopping me at the edge of a patch of blackberry canes.

Sylvia's eyes narrowed when she saw me. "Damien Dickens!" she spat out, turning my name into a curse. "Barney, this changes things."

"Not really." I saw something shiny fly through the air and land with a clank on the gravel at Sylvia's feet. "Cuff the girls together," he told her. "Ankles and wrists. We'll stash them in the shed for now and deal with them later."

"What about him?" She jerked her head towards me.

"I was thinking about the pond."

Sylvia shook her head rapidly from side to side. "No good," she said. "It's too shallow. And the neighbor's kids swim there. They'd spot him."

"Well, then Dickens and I will just take a walk through the woods to Grandma's house. Who knows," he added. "Maybe we'll meet a big bad wolf along the way."

Sylvia nodded. "The barn?"

"That's right. Go ahead and cuff 'em. They won't resist while I'm holding a gun to their hero's neck."

Sylvia positioned Susan and Millie back to back and cuffed Susan's left ankle to Millie's right. She did the same with their wrists, then cut the duct tape that had secured their hands behind their backs. When she was done, she grabbed their arms and turned them to face us. "Take a last look at your hero," she scoffed. Susan's eyes were wide with fear. Millie's face was pale and set. She was afraid, but in control. I caught Millie's eye and gave her a slight nod. She blinked a couple of times in reply and stood quietly, her body tense.

"You won't get away with this," I told Barnstable. "People know where I am. They'll find our bodies. Even if you kill us all, your game is up."

"Think you're the cat's pajamas, don't you," he sneered. "They won't find your body. There's an old septic tank at the back of the burnt-out barn next door. That's where you're heading. And maybe the ladies will be the victims of a fatal car accident. They were cautioned not to drive through Smuggler's Notch at night, but they did so anyway. Tragic."

"We're wasting time, Barney." Sylvia was shifting her weight impatiently from foot to foot.

"She's right, Dickens." Barnstable gave me an extra poke with the gun. "We're wasting time. Walk."

I walked straight into the brake of blackberry canes, keeping my head up, but my eyes cast down so that I wouldn't stumble. The gun barrel slipped away from my neck, and I sensed that Barnstable was caught in the cane brake. I spun around without lowering my arms and felt my right elbow connect with something hard. His head, I hoped. As I knocked him to the ground and grabbed for his gun hand, I caught a glimpse of Millie springing at Sylvia like a lioness, dragging Susan in her wake. Barnstable and I rolled over and over through the blackberries and onto the gravel driveway, both my hands gripping Barnstable's right wrist. His left hand tightened around my throat, as he tried to push me off and bring his gun to bear. We wrestled our way across the gravel and onto a large flat rock at the edge of the island of birch trees bounded by the circular driveway. As we rolled off the driveway, his right hand smashed into the rock. I heard a shot, followed by a groan and a dull thud, as the gun flew out of his hand and ricocheted into the trees. I managed to free my right arm and smashed my fist into Barnstable's jaw. His body went slack, and I lay on top of him for a few seconds, winded.

Shakily, I struggled to my hands and knees, then closed my eyes and shook my head to dissipate the fog that clouded my brain. When my vision cleared, I looked across the driveway and saw a body lying face-down in an expanding pool of blood.

Thirty-three

I pushed myself painfully to my feet and staggered across the driveway to where Millie and Susan were huddled on the gravel beside Sylvia's inert form. "Is she dead?" Susan's whispered question was laden with horror, leavened with a tinge of hope. I knelt down for a closer look. The stray bullet from Barnstable's gun had creased Sylvia's scalp, leaving a four-inch long gash that was bleeding profusely. I checked for a pulse at her neck; it was weak, but steady.

"She's alive," I reported. "She'll have one hell of a headache when she wakes up, and she's sure to need stitches, but I suspect the wound looks a lot more serious than it actually is." I took off my jacket and put it over Sylvia to keep her warm, then helped the girls to their feet.

They were still handcuffed together at the wrists and ankles like a couple of participants in a three-legged race at the Police Academy field day. They looked at me, then each other. Millie giggled nervously. "Oh, Dickie," she began. Then she looked at Sylvia's body and her voice dissolved into sobs. "W...we...were....soooooo...scared." I took both of them into my arms, and we held each other close as tears of relief bathed our faces and our clothing. Susan looked down at Sylvia. "It sounds terrible, but I'm almost sorry she's alive," she admitted in a tiny voice. "She put us all through the seven chambers of hell. First Celine, then Sethwick, then me. Even her brother," she added, jerking her head in Barnstable's direction. "It was all Sylvia's idea. She used whoever she could convince to do her dirty work."

"Let's get those bracelets off you," I suggested. "Then we can sit down and talk properly. Did Sylvia have the key?" They both shook their heads from side to side. "Then it's still on Barnstable. I'll go find it." I kissed them each lightly on the forehead. "Don't go anywhere. I'll be right back."

Before I could turn around, Millie gasped. "Dickie! Behind you." I spun and saw Barnstable stagger to his feet. He was wobbling, and there was a look of puzzlement on his face. But there was no mistaking the gun in his hand. It was the snub-nose Smith & Wesson .32 that he had taken from my pocket. And it was pointing straight at us.

I raised my arms high, elbows bent 90° and palms facing towards him. Making sure to keep my body between Barnstable and the women, I started easing forward. When I was about twenty feet away, he stopped me. "That's enough, Dickens," he said. "Don't come any closer." His face was pale, except where his skin bore smears of blackberry juice and the marks of a thousand tiny scratches from our earlier tussle through the brambles and across the gravel. His eyes were wild and darting, his gait unsteady as he edged cautiously towards the car that was parked in front of the garage. I could hear the faint whine of distant sirens. I had to distract him somehow - to delay him until the police arrived.

"OK, Barnstable," I said, standing my ground. "Have it your way." I started to lower my hands.

"Put them back up," he snapped. "Think you're so smart, don't you?"

I raised my hands high. "Smart enough to figure out that you killed Celine," I retorted. "But I still don't understand why."

"She was getting in our way."

"Our?"

"Syl and me. It was our father who started the company. It should have been ours. Sutherland stole it when he married our mother." His cheeks flushed dark red and his eyes snapped with the accumulation of a lifetime of anger. "It should have been ours," he repeated. "It should have been mine. Syl wanted out of the business, and I wanted in. So we joined forces to drive the company into bankruptcy. We bled out the cash and stashed it off-shore. I was going to come along - a knight in shining armor - and 'rescue' the company for ten cents on the dollar. Syl would end up with a pile of dough - that's all the company ever meant to her anyway - and I'd gain sole ownership of Sutherland Smokes. Celine got suspicious and started asking the wrong questions."

"So you killed her."

"We had no choice, once she stuck her nose into it."

"And you tried to frame me."

He shrugged. "You were a natural; Celine went to you for help. It might have stuck, too, if that pawn broker and his jerk of a nephew hadn't screwed it up."

"So you decided to eliminate Benny and Bruno."

"Not personally. I gave that job to Cosmo. Pity he botched the hit on the kid, though. And then the fool went and lost my gun. Fell out of his pocket into the septic tank when he dumped Benny's body."

"What was Gordon Sethwick's role in this little game of yours?"

"Sethwick?" Barnstable snorted, derision in his face and voice. "That fool? He knew nothing. But the dope was a useful dupe. He muddied the waters for us."

The sirens were getting louder now; Barnstable started edging sideways toward the car. I'd have to make my move soon. "I don't have time for this, Dickens," he said, as he pointed the gun at my chest. Then, suddenly, he jerked his head to the right as his peripheral vision detected movement - a family of wild turkeys parading in single file across the driveway. Instinct in overdrive, I sprinted towards him. Diving low to dodge a bullet, I wrapped my arms around his knees. He fell heavily, and I swarmed on top of him, wrenching the gun from his grasp.

I stood up, gun in hand, and dragged him to his feet just as a police patrol car appeared in the driveway, red lights flashing and siren screaming. I held the gun on Barnstable and watched as two officers got out of the car, drew their guns, and took up defensive positions behind the open car doors. "Freeze!" they shouted in unison, their guns pointed at me. "Drop your weapon, Mister. Hands on your head."

I tossed away the gun in the direction of the patrol car - and out of Barnstable's reach - and placed my hands on my head. The senior of the two officers rose out of his crouch and walked toward us, picking up the discarded weapon as he approached. He was a burly man, with a plain, no-nonsense air about him. His face was weathered and bore two small scars - one on his forehead, the other on his chin; his nose had an unnatural bump just below the bridge, as though it had been inexpertly set after a break. His name tag identified him as Sgt. L. LaPorte. "Walk slowly over to the patrol car, Mister," he instructed, his gun still pointing at me. "Put your hands on the hood and spread your legs."

"You have it all wrong, Sergeant," I turned my head to protest as the younger cop - Constable R. Tobias - began to frisk me. "Didn't Mr. Sethwick explain?"

"Don't know any Sethwick."

"Then, what are you doing here?"

"We got a call from a neighbor. Their kids were playing in the woods." Tobias gestured toward the nearby trees with one hand as he held me in place with the other. "They heard a shot, saw a ruckus, and ran home to call us. Good thing they did, too." He shoved me roughly against the hood of the car. "Stay put, Mister, if you know what's good for you. I'm not done with you yet." Tobias finished patting me down. "He's clean," he called out to his partner. "Fine," LaPorte replied. "Cuff him and stuff him. I'm almost done here."

LaPorte was talking to Barnstable. Getting his side of the story. I could see LaPorte nodding, his posture deferential, and I could imagine the scenario. Barnstable, the good guy protecting his client's property, being attacked by me. "He's lying to you," I shouted, shrugging off Tobias's grip on my arm. "Everything he's telling you is a lie." I pointed to Susan and Millie, who were trying to run across the driveway, still handcuffed together by the wrists and ankles. "Ask them."

"Mr. Dickens is telling the truth." By now, Susan and Millie were just a couple of yards away. "I'm Susan Sutherland, Sergeant." Susan was out of breath from the exertion of their three-legged race, but completely composed. "We danced together last year at the Harvest Festival."

LaPorte blinked twice and blushed. "Miss Susan! What's going on? Who are these people?" He paused and looked more closely at her. "Why are you handcuffed to this woman?"

Susan pointed her free hand in my direction. "This man is Damien Dickens, a Private Investigator," she explained. "He's working for me. I hired him to find the killer of my sister, Celine." She raised her other arm - the one that was still tethered to Millie. "Please get these cuffs off of us," she pleaded, and tilted her head to point at Sylvia, still lying unconscious. "That injured woman is my step-sister, Sylvia. She's the one who cuffed us together. He has the key, though," Susan added, gesturing in Barnstable's direction. "He and Sylvia are responsible for Celine's death. Mr. Dickens can explain everything."

While Tobias took care of freeing Millie and Susan, I gave LaPorte a précis of the Celine Sutherland affair, concluding with the flight to Stowe in Gordon Sethwick's plane, and the plan for Sethwick to take Arthur and his foster parents to the Morrisville police station. "Sethwick should have been here with the Morrisville police by now," I added. "He was supposed to leave the family at the station and bring help."

LaPorte looked over to Tobias, who was walking back over to the patrol car. "Call it in, Bob," he said, then turned to Barnstable, gripped him by the arm, and led him to the car. "OK, Mister," he instructed. "Put your hands on the hood and spread those legs."

LaPorte was efficient. Barnstable was searched, cuffed, and stuffed into the back of the patrol car by the time Tobias was done. "I've got back-up on the way," Tobias announced. "Also an ambulance for the injured woman. There's a problem, though." He paused and shook his head. "This Sethwick guy never made it to Morrisville."

Thirty-four

"Cosmo," I whispered. I looked at Susan - her pale face reflected my own anxiety - then turned to LaPorte. "We have to check out their house," I urged. "There's a bad dude on the loose. He might have ambushed Sethwick and the others." I jerked my head in Sylvia's direction as I pointed at Barnstable. "These two were after the boy. Cosmo was their accomplice in Celine's murder."

"I can't have you in the patrol car," LaPorte protested. "Not with him in custody in the back seat."

Susan walked over to the cherry-red Subaru still parked in front of the lodge and looked inside. "We can take my car, Damien," she called out. "Sylvia left the key in the ignition."

"We?"

"It's my car, after all."

"But..."

Susan held up her hand to stop me. "Millie and I are coming with you," she said. "Don't try to argue. There isn't time, and you won't change our minds. Besides," she added. "You might need our help."

I knew when I was licked. I turned to LaPorte. "I know the house. Want to follow me?"

"What's the address?"

"526 Worcester Loop. It's off Mansfield View."

He nodded. "I know the area. Let me lead until we turn onto Mansfield View. If there's traffic, the sirens will help. Once we're off Route 100, you take the lead." He turned to his side-kick. "You wait here until the ambulance and back-up team arrive, Bob. Then catch a ride with the ambulance to Copley Hospital in Morrisville."

"You want I should stay at Copley until ..."

"Until relieved, Bob. Sylvia Sutherland is a suspect in a murder investigation. Treat her as one. Make sure she gets proper medical care, but don't leave her unguarded. Stand post directly outside wherever she is - the ER cubicle, the OR, her room. Wherever they put her, you stick to her like chewing gum." With that, LaPorte walked over to his car and slid behind the wheel. "Let's go, Mr. Dickens. Time's a-wasting."

Millie and Susan were already in the Subaru, Susan riding shotgun in front. I got behind the wheel, started up the engine, and followed LaPorte up the driveway and down the hill into Stowe. We turned right onto Route 100 and raced unimpeded in the direction of Mansfield View, the patrol car's siren and flashing lights cutting a path for us through the relatively light late afternoon traffic. LaPorte negotiated the right turn onto Mansfield View and pulled over to allow me to take the lead up the road to Worcester Loop. I coasted to a halt at the side of the road just beyond the Hegarty's driveway. LaPorte pulled past me and parked a few feet ahead. We got out of the cars, closing the doors as quietly as we could, and huddled for a conference.

"The Hegarty's pick-up truck is gone," I told LaPorte. "That's the vehicle they were going to use to drive to Morrisville. There's no other car in the driveway."

"There still could be someone inside." He pointed at Millie and Susan. "You ladies stay here," he told them, "while we investigate."

"Wait a moment, Damien." Susan touched my arm, then reached through the open car window and into the glove compartment. "You might need this." She handed me a Colt pocket pistol. "It's loaded," she added. "Fires five rounds."

I thanked her with a silent hug and followed LaPorte as we approached the house from its blind side. Obeying his hand signals, I duck-walked left around the back of the house, while he went right. I peered cautiously through each window, but saw no signs of life. LaPorte and I met up just as I was about to look through the large living room window. Then we heard it - a whimpering bark coming from inside the house. "That's their dog, Portia," I whispered. "They were going to take her with them. Mary Hegarty insisted that she not be left behind."

"Cover me." LaPorte ran around to the front door and burst through into the house as I covered him from the living room window. "Clear!" he shouted. "Come inside, Dickens. Better see this."

I ran into the house and stopped in my tracks. Portia was lying on her side on the living room floor on top of a blood-stained braided throw rug. Her right ear had been shot off, and she had a bullet wound in her side. One of her hind legs was bent at an unnatural angle. She was alive and trying to growl and bark at us between whimpers. LaPorte stood shaking his head, then turned abruptly. "Stay here. I'll call this in from the car."

I squatted beside Portia and spoke gently to her. "I wish you could talk, girl," I told her. "I wish you could tell me what happened." She whimpered in reply, allowed me to stroke her head, and gave me a feeble lick. She rubbed her head against the rug, and I realized that she was trying to push something towards me. I reached down and picked up a small scrap of torn fabric. "Did you tear this off your attacker?" I asked her. "Is that what you're trying to tell me?" Portia replied with a feeble bark and closed her eyes. I sat back on my heels and stared at the scrap of cloth. It was a shirt cuff. A French cuff with the cufflink still in place - a green pearl set on a platinum oyster half-shell.

LaPorte came back inside the house, his face set; Millie and Susan were right behind him. "Your Mr. Sethwick has turned up," he told me. "I just got off the radio with the station in Stowe. They had a phone call from Mary Hegarty. It appears that Sethwick took Mrs. Hegarty, her husband and the boy at gunpoint and drove up the Mountain Road to Smuggler's Notch in their truck. He kicked the couple out of the truck at the Notch and continued north with the boy. Mr. and Mrs. Hegarty hiked back down the mountain until they could flag a passing car. The driver took them to the nearest phone. Sethwick has a pretty good head start. We think he's heading for the Canadian border. There are lots of back roads. In that truck, he could even go cross-country. We have roadblocks out. FBI has been notified - kidnapping is federal jurisdiction - and they're alerting the Canadians."

"Why would he head north?" I asked. "He has a perfectly good plane right here in Morrisville."

"Plane or no plane, our best information is that he's heading north." LaPorte turned to leave. "I have to take my prisoner in, then I'm heading for Copley Hospital in Morrisville to relieve my partner. You can follow me, if you like."

I turned to Susan. "Is there any way Sethwick could circle around from the Notch and get back to the airport?"

She nodded. "Easily. The Mountain Road meets Route 15 at Jeffersonville. He could cut east on 15, then pick up Route 100 just outside of Hyde Park. Or, if he wants to avoid the center of Morrisville, there's a back road - Cady's Falls - that bypasses Morrisville and meets Route 100 just a mile or so from the airport."

LaPorte stood listening, his foot tapping with impatience. "You go ahead," I told him. "I'm going to check out the airport."

"Suit yourself," he said with a shrug and left.

I looked at Millie, who was on her knees beside Portia, examining her wounds. "I think she has a chance," she reported. "I worked summers in a vet's office when I was in school. I think I can help her."

"Then you stay here and do what you can," I said and turned to Susan. "Fancy a ride to the airport? Arthur knows you. If I'm right, I may need your help." She nodded without speaking, and we ran back to the car. I executed a tight U-turn, sending dirt and gravel in several directions at once. In a couple of minutes, we were down the hill and back on Route 100, heading in the direction of the airport. The setting sun hung barely above the low treed ridge to our right. "Can Sethwick fly that plane even after dark?" I asked Susan.

She nodded. "I think so - if the plane is equipped with the necessary instruments. He's been flying for a long time. He's an experienced pilot."

"That's what I was afraid of." I put my hand on the horn and flashed my high-beam lights, passing vehicles as though they were standing still, a chorus of angry horns receding in my wake.

Susan pointed through the windshield. "That's the airport up ahead. I can see the end of the runway." She gripped my arm. "Damien, there's a plane taxiing in our direction toward the end of the runway. I think it's Seth's."

"Are you sure? How can you tell?"

"It's a tail-dragger. They're not too common. And the color scheme looks right - green and silver."

She squinted through the glass. "Yes," she said, after a pause. "It's Seth's plane. Oh, Damien." I could hear the tears in her voice as she choked out the words. "We're too late."

"Not if I can help it. Hang on!" I shouted as I wrenched the wheel to the right and bounced into a freshly plowed field. "I'm heading straight for the runway. Let's hope there's no fence." I wrestled with the steering wheel as we slipped and slithered through the soft dirt. The rain that had fallen the day before combined with recently spread manure to produce a slick, lumpy, slimy muck. Only the

Subaru's all-wheel drive kept us from becoming immobilized in the ruts and ridges left by the farmer's plow. At last, we reached the far end of the field, climbed a final berm, and emerged onto the tarmac. Sethwick must have spotted us driving across the field, because he turned into position for his take-off run short of the end of the runway. He was already rolling by the time we reached the paved surface, and I pressed the gas pedal to the floor to bridge the gap between us.

We caught up to the plane just as the tail wheel lifted off the ground. I kicked the Subaru into overdrive, shoved its front end under the tail, and plowed forward. The plane slewed to the right as the roof of the Subaru scraped the undercarriage of the fuselage. I jammed on my brakes and managed to keep the car on the tarmac; the plane looped around and came to rest - nose and left wing-tip in the ground and tail in the air - in a field of knee-high grass at the side of the runway.

I flung a terse "Stay here" at Susan, threw open my car door and raced over to the plane. The fuselage was intact, but the front landing strut had collapsed and there was a crack near the tip of the left wing. I smelled aviation fuel, and remembered that the fuel tanks were in the wings. Sethwick was slumped, unconscious, in his seat. I wrenched his door open and reached in to release his safety harness. Gravity took over, and he spilled out of the plane. I grabbed him under the armpits and dragged him to safety, then ran back to the plane. Susan was already there, looking frantic. "He's not here, Damien. Arthur isn't here," she told me.

"Get away from~here, you fool," I yelled at her. "I'll find him. This thing could blow at any time."

She held up her hand to silence me. "Wait," she said. "I think I just heard something. Listen."

We stood motionless, then heard a pattern of thumps, punctuated by muffled cries. "That's 'S.O.S.' It's coming from behind the rear seats." I remembered that Sethwick had mentioned a luggage compartment. "Look for a small door or hatch behind the passenger compartment."

"Here it is, Damien. Help me open it. It's stuck."

The smell of fuel was getting stronger. I ran over to Susan, and we managed to pry open the luggage hatch. I reached inside, grabbed Arthur by the collar of his shirt and pulled him free. Carrying the boy in my arms, I ran with Susan to the safety of the runway. I placed Arthur gently on the tarmac, left Susan to tend to him, and went over to check on Sethwick. He was still unconscious. A small cluster of mechanics and pilots had gathered. "Call 9-1-1," I said. "This man tried to kidnap that boy. We need the cops and an ambulance."

"Already on their way, Mister." I recognized Sethwick's mechanic, and nodded a curt acknowledgment. "Better move everyone back," I suggested. "The plane is leaking fuel. It could blow."

Thirty-five

I walked back over to Susan, who was kneeling on the runway, her arms wrapped around Arthur, comforting him. I stood behind them, placing a hand on her shoulder. "Help is on the way," I told her, my voice low. "Someone has already called 9-1-1." From where I stood, I could see an airport fire engine racing out to the crumpled plane, and watched as the crew began to spray the area with fire-retardant foam. At least we no longer had to worry about a fireball. We waited silently for a long moment, until we heard sirens approaching from both directions on Route 100. I saw an ambulance pull into the airport parking lot and gave Susan's shoulder a gentle squeeze. "I'd better go back over there," I told her, pointing to where Sethwick lay.

Two EMTs were already trotting over to Sethwick's inert body, a wheeled gurney piled with emergency equipment rolling between them. The cluster of onlookers parted to let them through. One of the white-coated medics knelt beside Sethwick; the other busied himself with their paraphernalia. "Pulse weak and thready," the kneeling medic called out. "BP eighty over fifty-five. Breathing shallow." By the time the police squad cars arrived, the medics had started an IV drip, attached a protective collar around Sethwick's neck, slid him onto a body board, and were lifting him onto the gurney.

I felt a tap on my shoulder. "Mr. Dickens? My orders are to bring you, Miss Susan, and the boy to Copley Hospital." I turned at the sound of Sgt. Laporte's familiar voice. Susan and Arthur already were standing beside him.

"What about Arthur's parents?"

"They arrived at the station just before I left. Someone will ferry them to Copley."

"And Millie?"

"I spoke to her by phone once Mary and Zeb Hegarty made it to the station. She's offered to stay with the dog. A neighbor has volunteered to take her and the animal to the emergency vet clinic in Hyde Park."

LaPorte cut off further conversation by herding us across the pavement, through a gate in the chain link fence that separated the parking lot from the tarmac, and over to his squad car. Ten minutes later, he pulled into an 'Emergency Vehicles Only' parking bay at Copley Hospital and shepherded us to the ER entrance. The hospital was a two-story red brick building devoid of any architectural flourishes. It looked as though it could house, at most, twenty-five or thirty patients. A handful of people were sitting in a small waiting room next to the ER. I could feel their angry stares boring into my back as LaPorte led us past them and into a private examining room. The ER team made fast work of checking us over: first Arthur, then Susan, then me. Except for a few minor abrasions, which they treated with antiseptic and covered with bandages, we were pronounced 'good to go.'

Mary and Zeb walked into the ER waiting area just as we were leaving the examining room. Arthur was the first to spot them. "Mom! Dad!" he cried, as he raced into their open arms.

Mary's eyes were spilling over with joy and relief, and Zeb's cheeks also were suspiciously moist. Mary looked up at me over Arthur's head. "Mr. Dickens, I don't know whether to curse you for leading that..." She hesitated, swallowed hard, and continued, "that man to our home, or whether to bless you for rescuing our boy."

"He had me fooled completely, Mrs. Hegarty," I admitted, shaking my head. "I don't know what else to say, except that I'm sorry. You have every right to be angry."

Mary shook her head. "I know you were doing what you thought was best," she said. "I'm not angry at you. Not any more. Not now that Artie's safe."

"I'd like to know what happened after I left your house. Do you feel up to talking?"

Zeb answered for her. "Mary's pretty tuckered out," he said. "And so is the boy. If one of the officers will agree to take them home, I'd be glad to talk to you."

"I think that's a good idea," Susan interjected, turning to Mary. "If it's all right with you, I'll come along too. I don't think you and Arthur should be alone."

We went outside together and said our good-byes. Zeb suggested that he and I head over to the coffee shop in the lobby. I followed him around the building to the main entrance. We purchased our coffee and found a table in a quiet corner. Instinctively, I sat with my back to the wall. We went through the usual silent ritual of adding cream and sugar to the aromatic brown liquid. I sipped my coffee, leaned back in my seat, and waited for Zeb to collect his thoughts. At last, he put down his styrofoam cup.

"Artie came downstairs just after you drove off," he began without preamble. "Mary introduced him to Sethwick, whose face went white. 'Celine,' he whispered, and put out his right hand. The boy walked over to shake hands, just like we've taught him when he's introduced to someone. But Sethwick grabbed his wrist and wouldn't let go. 'I'm your father, Arthur,' he said. 'I'm going to take you away with me. Far away.'

"Artie tried to free himself from Sethwick's grip; Mary moved to help him, and Sethwick pulled a gun. 'Stay away,' he shouted at her. 'I'm taking the boy. If either of you tries to interfere, I'll shoot him. If I can't have him, neither will you.' He had a strange look in his eyes, and we believed his threat. Mary stood still, but Artie continued to struggle. Then Portia sprang at Sethwick. He shot at the dog two or three times - it happened so fast I couldn't say for sure - and poor Portia just whimpered and collapsed on the floor. I think that Sethwick panicked then. He held the gun to Artie's head. Insisted that I tie the boy's arms and legs, and herded us out to the truck. He made me get behind the wheel, and told Mary to sit beside me. Sethwick climbed into the back seat with Artie. He ordered me to drive up the Mountain Road to Smuggler's Notch - threatened to kill both Mary and the boy if I refused. So I did what he said. He had me stop the truck at the narrowest point of the road - right at the Notch - told us to get out and stand back. Then he got behind the wheel and drove off north." Zeb stopped and took a sip of coffee. "Mary and I started back down the mountain towards Stowe on foot. We were able to flag a passing car, and the driver took us to the nearest phone so that we could call the police." He drained the balance of his coffee. "You know the rest."

Zeb heaved a heavy sigh, and I could see moisture gathering in the corners of his eyes. He fished a large, blue-and-white gingham handkerchief out of his pocket and blew his nose loudly, then covered his eyes with his left hand. I looked away and spotted LaPorte standing in the doorway to the coffee shop. He motioned to me; I excused myself and walked away.

"Sethwick's in a bad way," LaPorte said, tersely. "They need to operate. To relieve pressure on his brain. But he's regained consciousness and insists on seeing you before they take him to the O.R. Better hurry." I kept pace with LaPorte as we strode past doors marked 'X-ray' and 'Lab' and down to the end of the hall to the cubicle where Sethwick was being cared for. A nurse was hovering as I entered the tiny room; she made some notes on his chart, adjusted his IV, and retreated into the far corner of the room.

For a minute, the only sounds were the quiet hiss of a supplementary oxygen pump and the erratic ping of an

EKG monitor. Sethwick lay motionless on the bed, his eyes open. "Dickens?" His voice was weak; his breathing labored and raspy.

"Yes, it's me," I answered.

"Tell...boy...sorry." He was struggling to get the words out.

"Why did you do it, Sethwick?"

"Wanted...boy. Wanted... my son. Celine's son." He closed his eyes. "Tell...them...Tell....him..." He drew a single heavy breath, and the periodic ping from the heart monitor changed to a continuous piercing tone. The nurse hustled me out into the hall as an emergency response team burst into the room. The door swung shut behind them, and I waited in the hallway with LaPorte. Ten minutes later, the door opened. A doctor came out of the room, looked at us, and shook his head. LaPorte and I walked back to the coffee shop. Zeb was still sitting with his back to the door, his head now cradled in both hands. I tapped him on the shoulder and he looked up, startled. "Sethwick's dead," I reported. "We're taking you home."

By the time we arrived at the Hegarty house, Mary had settled Arthur in bed. The blood-stained rug had been removed from the living room floor, and Susan was busying herself in the kitchen, putting up a fresh pot of coffee and placing some slices of cake on a platter. LaPorte declined the offer of coffee and took his leave. "I have to get back to Copley," he said. "I still have a prisoner there. I want to interview Sylvia Sutherland as soon as she comes to."

Zeb walked over to Mary and put an arm around her. "Where's Artie?" he asked.

She put her finger to her lips. "Asleep. He went right to bed as soon as we heard from the vet clinic. Portia will pull through." Mary smiled in my direction. "Thanks to your friend, Millie," she added. "Doc Caplan said that Millie's patch job saved Portia's life." Mary teared up briefly, then changed the subject. "Sethwick?" she asked.

"Dead," I replied. "Woke up, said he was sorry, and died. You don't need to worry about him any more."

"I never understood what Celine saw in him." Susan broke into the silence that filled the room after my announcement. "But I didn't suppose him to be capable of murder."

"I don't think he was a party to Celine's murder," I told her. "I think that Sylvia and Barnstable used him as a decoy. He was up to his eyeballs in the embezzlement plot, though. He was the company's CFO; all the money flowed through him. I'll bet he set up a series of off-shore accounts and knew where every last dollar was hidden. Everything was going smoothly until Celine got suspicious. I know he tried to warn her off. She told me so."

"You don't believe he knew about the murder plot, then?" Susan interjected.

I shook my head. "Not in advance, no. I think he was still in love with her. He really believed at first that I had killed Celine. When he found out that Sylvia had connived with Barnstable to murder her, something inside him died. He kept his mouth shut, though. Probably figured he was in too deep. Then they kidnapped you and Millie," I said, looking at Susan. "Leaving him behind to take the fall alone. I turned up right afterwards and told him about his son. He must have figured that by helping me, he'd be able to recapture his lost love through Arthur. When the boy spurned him, Sethwick snapped. In his mind, he'd seen the two of them flying off into the sunset and living happily ever after on the embezzled company funds."

"But Arthur didn't want to go with him." Susan finished the story, reaching over to grasp Mary and Zeb's hands. "He wanted to stay with his real family."

Epilogue

Two Weeks Later

I checked my watch as I walked into Happy's. It was 5:30 on the dot. I looked around for Millie; didn't see her at first. As I scanned the room again, I spotted her in a booth in the back corner. Her hands were folded on the table, and her head was bowed. I walked over. "Hey, kid," I said as I slipped into the bench seat across from her. "This seat taken?"

She looked up at the sound of my voice, her welcoming smile belying the glisten of residual moisture in her eyes. "I was just thinking about the last time we met here," she whispered. "I know that I hurt you terribly."

I reached across the table and rested my hand on hers. "That's all behind us," I told her. "I'm famished. Let's order."

Millie grinned. "Already did. I knew exactly what you'd want."

I heard footsteps behind me and the cheerful clink of glasses dangling upside down on the necks of beer bottles. I looked up as Happy rested his tray on the table. "Two Sam Adams," he announced. "And your HappyBurger platters are right behind me."

For a few minutes, we busied ourselves with the ritual of ketchup, mustard and relish. I could see Millie watching me as I attacked my burger and fries. "What?" I asked. "Is there mustard on my nose?"

"Come on, Dick, tell me what happened at your meeting with Lt. Holmes and the D.A."

"Well, I'm back in business officially as a P.I." I replied. "Have my license and my gun permit back. Holmes followed up on my hunch about a second bullet. His team sifted about a cubic yard of sand in the area where her body was found and they finally located the slug that killed Celine. The bullet had blood and tissue residue on it that matched Celine's blood type. Turns out it was from the same gun that was used to kill Benny. Barnstable's gun. They found his gun in the septic tank up in Everettville, by the way."

"Did you see Bruno?" she asked. "What's happening with him?"

"The D.A. has decided not to press charges. Bruno is a free man." I helped myself to a few fries. "He wants to go to college, maybe even law school. He can afford it now. He has the money that Sophia put aside for him in addition to the trust fund that Barnstable set up for him."

"Barnstable set up a trust fund for Bruno?"

"Years ago. Isn't that a kicker? Turns out that Barnstable and Sophia had an affair in college. Bruno was the outcome. Barnstable never acknowledged him officially, but had a lawyer set up a fund to support Sophia and give Bruno a start. Sophia told me the story when Bruno was in the ICU, but she referred to her lover as 'Barney' and I didn't make the connection right away."

"And Cosmo? What will happen with him."

"Ahhh, Cosmo. He was picked up at the airport, trying to board a flight for Mexico City. He's turned state's evidence as part of a plea bargain. Cosmo worked for Barnstable for a few years - part go-fer, part chauffeur, and part enforcer. Turns out that Barnstable had a little loan shark business on the side. Cosmo was his collector."

"And his accomplice."

"Right. Barnstable wanted to throw smoke - like a squid squirting ink to confuse its attacker. He told Cosmo to recruit Bruno as a front man."

"You mean for stuff like delivering the note to Celine at the ball?"

"Yeah, and making like a cop on the Boardwalk after Cosmo slugged me from behind."

"But why kill Benny?"

"Benny got scared when he realized that he might be an accessory to a murder. He threatened to blow the whistle on Cosmo." I stood up. "Enough questions." Millie started to rise, but I waved her back down. "Slide over." I sat down on the bench beside her. She looked at me, her forehead crinkling in puzzlement. "I have something to show you," I said. I reached into my pocket, drew out a small velvet-covered box, and placed it on the table next to her HappyBurger platter. "This is for you." Millie looked at me; her mouth was moving, but nothing was coming out. "Well, aren't you going to open it?"

She picked up the box and lifted the lid. Inside, nestling on a bed of velvet, was a ring, set with a perfect green pearl resting on a miniature platinum oyster half-shell. Millie's eyes moistened. "Oh, Dickie," she breathed. "It's beautiful."

I took the box from her and removed the ring. "Let's see how it fits." Millie extended her right hand, and I slapped it playfully. "Not that one, silly. The other hand." Her eyes and mouth formed a triangle of perfect circles as she held out her left hand for me to slip the ring onto her finger.

"Dickie." Her voice caught. She swallowed and began again. "Dickie, are you sure?"

"Absolutely," I replied, leaning over to take her in my arms. "Here's looking at you, kid," I whispered as I touched my lips to hers.

—-THE END—-

Made in the USA
Coppell, TX
09 August 2020